THE BLACK BONES GARDEN

A. Torres Salabarías

Jorge Alonso

Title: The Black Bones Garden.

Authors: Jorge Alonso and A. Torres Salabarrías, 2024.

Illustrations: A. Torres Salabarrías.

Cover: Fermín Vega.

ISBN: 978-65-01-18349-7

Presentation

How do you react when the foundations that support your world view are shaken? What do you do when unknown paths, that can lead you to the satisfaction of all your desires or to the annihilation of your being and of all Creation, open before you? How do you act when powers that escape the reach of reason and the limits of imagination rise up against you?

The protagonists of the stories contained in this book, face dilemmas like these. In this anthology of Cosmic Horror and suspense stories, the authors draw on the Lovecraftian context of the Cthulhu Mythos to weave adventures that challenge the characters' sanity. In them, extraterrestrial beings, hidden knowledge, cursed books and primordial entities lurk with their seductive and terrifying powers.

We hope, dear reader, that you enjoy reading this book.

To those who, at the limits of hope,
fight in the darkness.

SUMMARY

ABOUT THE AUTHORS

A. Torres Salabarías is a young writer, a fan of Science Fiction and Horror.

Besides his work as a writer, he also works in the creation of cartoons, illustrations and comics of various genres.

In this work he ventures into literature with stories of the Cosmic Horror subgenre.

Jorge Alonso is a fan of science fiction, fantasy and horror literature and a great lover of the classics. He has bachelor's degrees in accounting and computer science and a master's degree in computer science and knowledge management.

He has collaborated with Fermín Vega in the fantasy saga Auroria, The Untold Chronicles.

In this book he experiments in the Horror genre with the aim of telling entertaining stories that transport the reader to a world far from the daily routine.

PROLOGUE

In the first years of the second decade of the 21st century, the period in which I write these lines, there has been a substantial increase in the amount of "content" based on or referring to the work of the American writer Howard Phillip Lovecraft.

The vast majority of creators of this "content" follow the same *modus operandi*. First, they perform the ritual of firing a round of criticisms of the author's ideas, because these ideas deeply hurt the delicate sensibilities of today day and age, strategically forgetting that as Lovecraft aged and matured, his way of thinking also changed and become more moderate. After the seemingly mandatory rite of declaring that H.P. was a true abominable monster and making it clear that they are virtuous and absolutely do not agree with him; they proceed to voraciously collect the juicy fruits that have sprouted from the seeds planted by the creator of the Cthulhu Mythos.

For over a hundred years, critics have been bleeding out inkwells and pounding keyboards in order to remark the flaws in style, the lack of maturity, depth and literary quality of Lovecraft's works. However, the author's prose has the indisputable ability to create a unique, enveloping atmosphere that captures the reader in the first lines and leads him, masterfully playing with his emotions, to surprising and unexpected endings.

The stories of the writer from Providence have the ability to kidnap us from our routine and gradually drag us towards a reality in which the thin veneer of normality, when torn away, exposes bizarre and terrible beings for whom Humanity, with all its creations and conflicts, are completely insignificant, nothing more than a mere toy, a trivial piece in a game whose scale and complexity we are unable to understand.

As a true master of his craft, Lovecraft managed to combine various elements, such as the classics of universal literature, gothic horror stories, scientific knowledge, his encyclopedic knowledge of the English language, the many vicissitudes he suffered in his life, and his own world views in the crucible of his fervent imagination. As a result, we have the monumental pieces of the subgenre that, in my opinion, is one of the most difficult to master: Cosmic Horror.

In this subgenre, the source of fear is not physical harm or torture; nor, as has been more or less consecrated by visual representations, giant, tentacled monsters, much less the damnation of the immortal soul. No, the driving force behind the discomfort, apprehension, and terror is the gradual discovery of truths that crush the most fundamental foundations that support the presuppositions, heuristic schemes, and moral structure of the characters in these stories.

Lovecraftian protagonists, in general, reach an end worse than physical death; they suffer the loss of reason, sanity and identity, the most precious assets from the humanist point of view, which was the dominant current of thought in the era in which Lovecraft lived. In this way, the philosophy that sustains Cosmic Horror frontally attacks anthropocentrism, removing the human being from the center of creation and relegating it to an unbearable insignificance.

Although Lovecraft's literary works have attracted a growing number of admirers and have exerted an enormous influence on a great number of writers, screenwriters and creators of various forms of entertainment; they had very limited success with the general public during the author's lifetime. The reasons for this failure are often cited as the complex vocabulary of his works and the eccentric complexity of the ideas and themes addressed.

Perhaps the most interesting theme implicitly presented in Lovecraftian stories is the importance of knowledge. The search for knowledge can be either the path to irremediable doom or the access to the very few tools capable of providing the opportunity to offer some resistance to the forces of the unknown.

Since Lovecraft always encouraged the use of his creations, especially those related to the Cthulhu Mythos, the authors of this book have decided to make this small tribute to the work of this great writer.

We offer readers a collection of Cosmic Horror stories. In our stories, the characters face eccentric and terrifying situations that push them to the limits of their abilities. Our goal is to provide you with a path for entertainment and, perhaps, some jump scares. Enter this path at your own risk.

Good luck!

JOURNEY IN THE DARK

A huge reddish flash filtered through the windshield. It was so intense that it made Yenny close her golden eyes, and she almost lost control of the car. The first crazy thought that occurred to the young woman was that, somewhere not too far away, a nuclear bomb had exploded, or a meteorite had fallen. With a grimace of her small mouth, she dismissed the idea. In those places forgotten by God and by men nothing exciting ever happens.

Since there was no rumble or sign of shock waves to support the young woman's theories, Yenny turned the radio dial to catch up on any news about some catastrophe in the region. The stations only broadcast frivolous programs to entertain the night listeners. Nothing about any event that would break that tectonic routine.

The girl was amused by the idea of being the only witness to the intense flash that had drawn the rounded silhouettes of the distant mogotes on the horizon of the infinite plain.

In that region there was no shortage of stories of strange things, such as mysterious lights that were seen in the sky after midnight. According to the story, every time one of these lights was seen, the next day they would always notice that some cattle was missing.

The truth is that the mystery lasted very little and generally the animal was found a few days later, lost in the thick *marabú* bushes or fallen into one of the many *cacimbas* that were so abundant in those places. Yenny suspected that the locals invented all this to combat the endless boredom of living there.

“When I get home, I'll talk to Mom about it, after all, the old woman knows everything” she thought.

The only oasis of entertainment was the stories her mother told her. That old woman had an encyclopedic knowledge of the world. She had often seen her advising peasants on how to solve a huge variety of things.

Yenny often wondered why her mother, being such a cultured and well-prepared person, had gone to live at this end of the world, dragging her with her.

In her modest house, almost on the outskirts of the village, one of the rooms was occupied by a very well-stocked library. Yenny had had access to all the books in the collection since she was very young. Well, almost all of them.

There was a very rare book that only her mother could read and that she jealously kept in an ornate metal box closed with an old-looking padlock. One time, when she was not looking, the box was left open, at the mercy of the curiosity of the then little Yenny. And the little girl did not let the opportunity pass her by.

As she recalled, the volume was quite old, yellowed and worn looking. The title had words that made her think of some disgusting contagious disease. It was something like... "*Diarem*" ... perhaps "*Viarem Carcosa*".

—"*Viarium quae Carcosa*", —the young girl murmured almost unconsciously.

Anyway, her mother had caught her before she could open the book. After an exemplary scolding, she gave her a two-week detention and hid the object in such a way that she never saw it again.

Yenny didn't even insist on looking for it, as she spent two months having vivid nightmares about the damn thing. In her dreams, unspeakable monsters appeared to her, coming out of the book itself. The most sinister of the entities was what she described as "A faceless old man covered in yellow rags."

The young woman pushed away all those memories. That was the past and she wanted to think only about the future.

The next year she will enroll in the University. Needless to say, her mother had not been at all pleased when the girl expressed her irrevocable desire to escape from that morass of endless boredom and see the rest of the world. For a while the old woman was very upset, but finally she accepted it.

"Even though the old lady is a little overprotective, she always makes me happy" thought the young woman, smiling.

He tuned the radio to a frequency that played relaxing pop music and hummed along to the songs transmitted by the device while trying to glimpse anything beyond the beam of the headlights, trying to have a vague hobby to distract himself with.

It was quite dark out there. Only the steel shell moving at high speed separated she from the darkness that completely swallowed up the bushes on both sides of the road. Darkness that the car's headlights were responsible for dissipating for a limited space, like a kind of lighthouse pointing its beam of light through the waves of irregular aromatic plants bordering the narrow strip of asphalt along which it advanced.

He had only recently obtained his driving license, and it was his first time driving on that desolate road late at night. He thought it would be very unpleasant to have an accident or have the car break down in a place like that, in the middle of nowhere.

Lost in her thoughts, she took a while to notice the obstacle in the road. She slammed on the brakes violently and the tires screeched on the asphalt. The girl's car stopped just a few meters from the vehicle stopped in the middle of the road.

The way was completely blocked. Yenny honked her horn a few times but got no response. Reluctantly, she pulled a flashlight from the glove compartment and got out of her vehicle to investigate the situation.

She unlocked the door and walked out.

—Hello, is anyone there? —she asked out loud as she walked cautiously.

With a jump scare she noticed something in front of her.

It appeared to be a man sitting on the pavement. He was laying on the asphalt, half hunched over, not speaking or even moving. The powerful light from the flashlight illuminated the figure's back, but his head was bent over his chest at an angle that sent shivers down the young woman's spine.

The situation was becoming somewhat unsettling. In contrast to the cozy interior of the car, it was cold outside, too cold for that time of year.

Yenny noticed the unfathomable silence and tranquility of the surroundings. She was used to the usual sounds of the countryside. That's why it seemed very strange to her not to hear even the chirping of a cricket. The mere presence of that individual seemed to have frightened every living being for a good distance.

On the sides of the road there were nothing, but immense expanses of pastures half taken over by *marabuzales* and sporadic royal palms. Any sign of civilization was several kilometers away.

Under these circumstances, Yenny thought that she might have to tow the unfortunate man's car to the nearest service station. However, she was not attracted by the idea of being in the same space as that strange individual.

—Sir, are you okay? Do you need help? —she asked.

But there was no response. The mysterious figure didn't even turn to look at the young woman. After repeating the question, there was a brief moment of silence until the man answered very seriously with an almost severe tone.

—I need to find it, —he said.

Something about the man's voice struck Yenny as very strange. Maybe it was the kind of buzzing sound it made when he spoke, something akin to the soft flutter of a bumblebee's wings.

What had this man lost on the dark pavement? Had he perhaps stepped out of his car and dropped his keychain?

On the sides of the road there were nothing, but immense expanses of pastures half taken over by marabuzales and sporadic royal palms. Any sign of civilization was several kilometers away.

Several things about the situation didn't sit right with the young woman. It was like a mental puzzle that, instead of coming together, was falling apart piece by piece, leaving behind many gaps and quite intriguing empty spaces.

The next piece to suddenly dislodge was the way the man's car was parked. The vehicle was blocking the entire road, preventing passage.

Feeling it would be extremely dangerous to turn her back on the increasingly suspicious stranger, Yenny walked backwards toward the stopped car.

She tried to push the vehicle to clear the way, but her hand found no solid surface, and she lost her balance.

The supposed car was nothing more than an illusion. A kind of faint glow was emanating from the ground, projecting the image of the car. When she waved her hand through the mirage, the light flickered like a glitch on a phone screen.

"A hologram? But how is that possible? I know those things are common now, but I've never heard of one so perfect. What the hell is going on here?" the young woman thought.

The fragile calm she had been holding onto shattered like a puzzle struck with a mallet, with all its pieces scattering to the corners of her mind. Her instincts screamed at her to flee as fast as she could.

The man stood up with an impossible leap. At a terrifying speed, he walked over and planted himself in front of Yenny. The girl felt a knot in her stomach when the light from her flashlight illuminated the stranger's face. Something was very wrong with that face.

The features were surreal, artificial. It was like a morbid mask covering God-knows-what deranged features. It was as if this macabre individual had ripped someone's face off and draped the loose skin over his own.

—I need to find it, —he whispered with a horrid buzzing voice, without even moving his lips. —She has it. I must get it. You are the way. You will lead me to it.

The man spoke the words with just the right volume and exact tone to elicit from Yenny the most primal scream of terror.

This terrifying individual did not have good intentions.

The girl ran, terrified, toward the only possible refuge at that moment: her car.

Covering the short distance to her car took enormous effort. It felt like running in a nightmare, where no matter how fast you move, you just don't get anywhere.

After what felt like an eternity, she managed to reach her car. Her trembling hands opened the door.

Seated in the driver's seat, ready to floor the gas pedal and not slow down until she got home, she was repulsively shocked to realize that "it," which had been grotesquely staggering after her, had caught up and was trying to open the door. Yenny hit the lock with a frantic slap.

The abominable monster disguised as a human leaned toward the window. That cosmic aberration peered into the car. The movement made the nauseating mask fall onto the glass. The object made a disgusting sound and slid down the surface, leaving a trail of sticky slime.

Yenny screamed again.

What was tormenting her was a being unlike anything existing in this world. It had no eyes or any other facial features. It was a repugnant alien creature with a deformed mass of reddish tissue full of protrusions where the face should have been.

The young woman wept, begging the car to take her away as soon as possible. But the engine wouldn't respond to the continuous, frantic turns of the ignition key.

The horrible being on the other side of the glass seemed to enjoy the screams, cries, and frantic pleas of its victim, whose only refuge had turned into a trap. The terrified girl's frantic reactions were amusing and even pathetic to the cold perception and crude intelligence of that entity, born from the abyss of the cosmos.

This alien entity may have been created with malevolent intentions under the glow of a titanic red sun. Perhaps it had come from beyond the orbit of icy Yuggoth. What was its goal? Did it want to study or maybe even consume other life forms, abducting them and dragging them into the depths of the galaxy?

Tired of the game, the aberrant creature reached for its waist and apparently activated some device, as the car door, in which Yenny had placed all her trust and security, simply ceased to exist. The girl screamed again as unimaginable dark appendages extended from the creature's body, touching her skin and beginning to wrap around her.

Her scream of terror was lost among the thorns of the marabou bushes, under the cold, indifferent light of the stars.

—I need to find it, —the horrid buzzing voice repeated. —She has it. I must get it. You are the way. You will lead me to it.

It was already past one o´clock in the morning, and the girl still hadn't come home.

The mother paced back and forth, constantly glancing at the clock at increasingly shorter intervals. She was very anxious and nervous. Yenny was her only daughter, and the thought of something happening to her terrified her.

Just imagining her beloved daughter alone in the dark at that hour out there sent chills down her spine. So, when the doorbell rang, she ran to the door.

She felt immense relief in her chest when she saw her through the peephole.

—Do you think this is an appropriate time to be getting home, young lady? —she said, putting her hands on her hips as she opened the door. —You've made me so worried; you know? What's wrong with you? Why aren't you reacting? Don't you have anything to say?

—You taught me not to interrupt when grown-ups are talking, right? —the girl replied with a coldness that left her mother stunned.

—Yes... That's true, but I expected some sort of reaction from you. A protest or, I don't know, an explanation, no matter how absurd. What's wrong with your voice? Are you sick or something?

—No, Mother.

—Look, I know you're at an age where you want to live every moment and experience to the fullest. I understand that sometimes impulsive decisions make you lose track of time. Believe me, I went through that phase too. But please, darling, try to learn to respect the curfews I set for you to come home. It's for your own good. Okay?

In response to her mother's gentle words, who raised her hand to tenderly caress her expressionless face, the girl tried to smile. The result was something much closer to a grimace of pain.

The horrible and forced grimace on the small mouth sent a chill of repulsion down the woman's spine. She backed away from that figure, slowly retreating until she bumped into a small table against the wall.

—Oh, my God, —the woman said in horror. —You're not my daughter.

Stealthily, hiding the movement with her body, she activated a hidden mechanism in the table and pulled out a long object wrapped in dark fabric from a secret compartment. Without taking her eyes off what appeared to be her beloved daughter, she searched with trembling fingers for one of the ends of the wrapping.

The eerie imitation managed to say dryly, in a voice that seemed to buzz from deep in its throat:

—I need to find it, —the disconcerting voice whispered. —You have it. I must get it.

—What have you done to my daughter, monster? —the woman murmured, unwrapping the object behind her back. In her golden eyes, a fierce flame of rage burned. —I swear, if you've harmed her, you'll pay in a way that has never crossed your twisted and disgusting mind. Where is my daughter?

—She was only the way. Just a means to get to it.

With incredibly quick movements for someone her age and weight, the woman brought her arms in front of her body, adopting a fighting stance. Her hands held a long black dagger. Strange symbols, glowing intensely in red, ran along the blade of the weapon.

—You have it. I must get it. —The being with Yenny's appearance repeated. Its hand began to move toward its waist.

MISSING

—Come on, Big Mouth, you know I would never hurt anyone, much less her! —The young man locked up shouted while desperately clutching the cell bars.

—I already told you to address me as Sheriff Pérez. We received orders to keep you here until the agents from the provincial capital arrive. They will take your official statement, —the police officer responded as he put away the cell key and added in a quieter, more personal tone, —Cairós, man, what did you all get into?

—I don't know, Big Mouth, I don't know, but I swear I'm going to find out.

—I already told you, it's Sheriff Pérez, —the policeman said as he walked away from the small cell and headed toward the station's door. —And you're staying there until we get orders to release you, —his voice had returned to a tone of authority.

In all the countless times Cairós had passed by the small police station in the *batey* where he was born and raised, he had never imagined he would one day be sitting on the concrete bench in the only cell of the place. The additional fact that the one keeping him there was none other than Big Mouth, his school mate from kindergarten through high school, and who was now the Sheriff in charge of the place, was something the young man couldn't have imagined even in his worst nightmares.

What exasperated Cairós the most was that he had voluntarily gone to the station precisely to alert Big Mouth, now Sheriff Pérez, about his deep concern for Lucía. And that idiot had tricked him, making him enter the cell and locking him up, saying they had received a call from the provincial capital to find him and keep him under arrest until further orders.

Cairós violently shook the crude rebar gate while shouting a string of insults at his former schoolmate. After venting a bit, he sat back down on the uncomfortable bench. What gnawed at him inside was the insidious idea that while he was sitting on the cold concrete doing nothing, Lucía might be in danger.

As the dusty air of the place began to turn red with the approaching dusk, Cairós heard the sound of a car parking on the loose gravel in front of the station. He strained to listen but couldn't make out the words spoken in the station's lobby.

—Hey, stop wasting time and start doing something to...

A figure appeared in the hallway leading to the cell. It was a thin man, slightly taller than average. He wore leather loafers that, despite evident intensive use, were meticulously clean. He was dressed in synthetic fabric pants, in a color somewhere between brown and yellow. A light yellow short-sleeved guayabera with the expected collection of pens in the chest pocket completed the outfit. The newcomer had a well-groomed mustache, though a bit thicker than necessary, which matched his neat haircut and bland side-parted hairstyle. Over his eyes, he wore dark, papillon-style glasses with iridescent lenses and gold frames. In his hands, he held an agenda with some embossed logo on its dark leather covers.

Cairós felt a vague sense of discomfort. He remembered feeling that way during military service when some guys who identified themselves as Military Police investigators conducted some "interviews" about the disappearance of three recruits, who were later found to have fallen into a sinkhole.

—A chair, please, —the newcomer requested with a completely apathetic voice.

Sheriff Pérez brought the piece of furniture and placed it diligently in front of the closed gate. He made a timid attempt to stay in the room, but after a cold glance from the mustached man, he left.

The man sat rigidly in the chair and crossed one leg to use it as a support for his agenda. Without removing his glasses, he flipped through some pages with long, nicotine-stained fingers.

He slowly took out a pack of cigarettes from a pocket and lit one using an old-fashioned kerosene lighter with a bronze body. With a skillful move that snapped the lighter shut with a metallic click, he extinguished the flame. Without looking at him, he offered the pack to Cairós, whose initial discomfort had given way to growing impatience.

Coughing from the smoke, the young man declined the offer with a shake of his head.

—Look, instead of wasting time here, we should...—Cairós began to say, but the apathetic voice of the mustached man interrupted him.

The newcomer started reading from his agenda.

—Cairós Díaz Aragón, twenty-two years old, in your fourth year of chemical engineering at Central University, and native of...—he paused to look around, —this town.

The young man inside the cell nodded in agreement and started speaking again.

—I'm not important, the one who might be in danger is...

—Lucía Clara Jara Caraballo, twenty-two years old, in her fifth year of fine arts at the Academy of Fine Arts, and also a native of this town, —the man in the chair released a large cloud of smoke through his narrow nose, lifted his gaze from the pages, and looked directly at Cairós.

Someone flipped a switch, and a dim incandescent lamp flooded the room with an anemic yellowish light.

—Can you explain to me, —the man continued apathetically, —what makes you think that your friend Lucía might be in danger?

The young man, without getting up from the bench, straightened his back, rested his elbows on his knees, brought his face closer to his interlocutor, and stared at him. He saw his own face reflected twice in the lenses, tinted yellow by the lamp's glow. He took a deep breath and began to speak.

—I've known Lucía since we were kids. In fact, I think the first memory I have in my mind is seeing her at a birthday party, wearing a white dress with golden ribbons in her hair. She, ignoring the party, was trying to pick a bunch of *romerillo* flowers. The stems wouldn't give, so I went over, pulled out the flowers, and handed them to her. She looked at me with her big honey-colored eyes and asked, "Do you want to be my friend forever?" At that moment, I had no idea what "forever" meant, but I said yes. We must have been about four years old at the time.

The man in the chair had taken out one of the pens from his guayabera pocket and seemed ready to take notes if something of interest came up. For the moment, he hadn't written anything.

—We always played together, although her family was very strict with her, and from a very young age, her parents made her study for many hours on topics that were kind of... —Cairós paused, —eccentric.

—Can you define what you mean by "eccentric"? —asked the man in the chair as he lit another cigarette.

—Well, for starters, foreign languages. Her dad is British or something like that, and she learned to speak English almost alongside Spanish. Later, they taught her French, German, and even Latin and Ancient Greek. At fifteen, she could read an ancient Bible in her house library, which she said was in Aramaic.

—Was the family religious? —the mustached man asked while writing something in his agenda.

Cairós shifted uncomfortably on his hard seat.

—I don't think they were necessarily religious; they were more like bibliophiles. They had a huge library with very old and odd-looking books.

—Did you ever read those books?

—I don't have the same knack for languages as Lucía. She even tried to teach me something, but I'm more into numbers than letters.

—But did you see what was in them?

—Mainly the pictures. Lucía loved looking at the images in those big old books and drawing them. When we were kids, we spent a lot of time playing and drawing, lying on the floor of her home library. Lucía had a particular liking for riddles, puzzles, word games, and that kind of stuff, but what she truly loved was drawing. Everyone was surprised when, instead of pursuing a career in English Language or Philology, she went to the Academy of Fine Arts. I wasn't surprised; I always knew her true passion was drawing and painting.

—What was Lucía's relationship with her family like?

—They got along quite well, but when her father used his Spanish citizenship to leave the country and Lucía didn't want to go with them, they had serious arguments.

—Wasn't her father British? How did he have Spanish citizenship?

Cairós scratched his head.

—Look, I'm not sure about the details, but it seems that Lucía's relatives were aristocrats who emigrated from the British Isles to southern Spain. From what I understand, the family's original surname was Hare or O'Hare, and they changed it to Jara, I think to make it sound more Spanish. They even have a coat of arms; it's red with a black hare, it's in a mosaic on the floor of their home library...

The man in the chair took quick notes in his agenda. Seeing that the young man wasn't too keen on continuing, he took the initiative again.

—Why did Lucía pass up the chance to leave the country and separate from her family?

—Well, around that time, she was very happy with her career, and also... our friendship had turned into something more...—Cairós felt the mustached man's silence probing him. —We were already dating, — the young man explained.

—Although the separation from her family saddened her for a while, she got over it, and we were very happy. I think it was the happiest year of my life.

The sound of the pen tip running over the paper of the agenda dominated the room until the man in the chair lit another cigarette. The smoke gathered in an ethereal cloud on the stained ceiling.

—But that happiness ended, didn't it? —the apathetic voice of the mustached man questioned, —what happened?

—Everything started going wrong when she began her internship at the provincial museum. Considering her skills, they called her to catalog and restore some old books that were in the building's basement. Lucía's work mainly involved reproducing the engravings in those big old books because many were in such bad condition that they couldn't even be scanned without crumbling to dust. One day she came home all excited. She told me that among the collection she was working on, there was a very old volume, which she had read about in her father's books, but they had never found a copy. The next day, she was going to start working on that book.

—Do you remember what the book's title was?

—At the time, I didn't pay much attention, —Cairós continued, lost in thought, ignoring his interlocutor's question. —The truth is that I almost ignored what Lucía was saying because I was focused on studying for my Organic Chemistry final exam. That was the beginning of the change. As she worked on that damn thing, she became more and more obsessed with its contents. She started writing notes in increasingly strange languages and drawing weird symbols in her notebook. More than once, she woke me up talking in her sleep in languages I didn't even recognize. Now I realize I should have done something then...

—The title of the book...—the man in the chair insisted.

—Huh? —Cairós responded with a slight start, having gotten lost in his thoughts. —What?

—Do you remember the title of the book Lucía was working on?

—"*Viarium quae Carcosa*", —Cairós replied. —It means something like "Of the Paths that Lead to Carcosa" or something like that.

—You told me you're not good with languages, and it turns out you speak Latin.

—I barely speak our language, —the young man replied. —Lucía told me that was the approximate translation of the title. She spent weeks constantly talking about that damn book, about hidden clues leading to a marvelous city where she could finally find everything she wanted to know, or things like that. I was too busy with my final exams, so I didn't pay much attention.

Cairós buried his face in his hands and seemed to sob. The man in the chair watched him closely through his gold-tinted lenses.

—The last time I saw her was three days ago. She was emaciated and disheveled. When she hugged me, I noticed she hadn't bathed in quite some time. I could barely understand what she was saying because she was speaking in an unintelligible mix of languages. She had her backpack on and insisted she was going on some kind of trip. I thought she would come back here. But when I went by her house, she wasn't there. I couldn't find any trace of her. I came to the police for help, and you guys just locked me up here.

The mustached man, with his usual slowness, removed the nearly burnt-out cigarette from his lips. The flame was already dangerously close to the bushy mustache. He flicked the butt to the ground with the others and said,

—What else do you know about the book?

—I don't know anything else about that damn book. The first time I heard about it was a few months ago when Lucía started talking about it, and as I already told you, I didn't pay much attention to her comments, but I imagine it has something to do with her change in behavior.

—Are you sure you're not hiding anything from me?

—I'm not hiding anything! You guys are the ones wasting time while Lucía is in danger, —the young man, agitated, stood up abruptly and grabbed the gate with force.

—How are you so sure that Lucía is in danger? —the man in the chair asked impassively.

Cairós calmed down and leaned against the gate. He lowered his head and replied in a low voice,

—As I already told you, I went to Lucía's house this morning. Since we started dating, she gave me a key. At first, I thought no one had been there in some time. However, on the library floor, around the family coat of arms mosaic, there was something... written in what looked like dried blood. *"Memento quoniam in crepusculo lepus cito currit."* I remember that was part of a little song Lucía's dad used to sing to her when she was a child; it was like a family tradition.

The young man paused, but he felt the yellow-tinted lenses staring at him, forcing him to continue. He took a deep breath and kept talking.

—Lucía explained to me that it means something like "remember that at dusk the hare runs fast", because, in the past, her ancestors were accused in their home region of doing horrible things like witchcraft, cannibalism, and making pacts with demons from the center of the Earth. That's why they fled, like the hare. She used to tell me she would love to know more about her ancestors' history. To search for more information on the subject. But her father always told her that some things are better left forgotten in the past because, even after so much time, they can still bring ruin and doom. And now she's missing...

Cairós, with a defeated look and his head down, kept his forearms hanging out of the cell.

The man in the chair placed a new cigarette between his lips and pulled out the bronze lighter.

Suddenly, the lights went out. The place was plunged into abysmal darkness.

Before he could react, the young man felt his arms being pulled outward with immense force. His face was violently pressed against the bars. He heard a terrifying voice whispering in his ear.

—Where did they take the book? Where is the seed? Don't try to deceive me, because I'll know right away if you're lying.

—I don't know what you're talking about. I've never seen the damn book. And what the hell is that seed?

A faint explosion was heard in the distance. The force holding Cairós against the bars suddenly disappeared. The young man backed up, gasping, until he hit the bench and fell hard on the concrete.

The incandescent lamp flickered back on. The man was still sitting in his chair. He didn't seem to have moved. He lit the lighter and brought the flame to the cigarette. He took a deep drag and released a considerable puff.

Sounds of commotion began to come from outside. A siren wailed in the distance.

With great slowness, the man in the chair put his pen back in his pocket and closed the agenda. He threw the rest of the cigarette to the ground and crushed it with his foot.

—I have no obligation to tell you this, but you seem genuinely concerned about Lucía. The provincial museum reported the disappearance of a very old volume that Lucía Jara was working on restoring. Also, a rare jewel belonging to the collection of an ancient and, in the past, wealthy family from the provincial capital is also missing. With the information we have so far, we can conclude that Lucía Clara Jara Caraballo is responsible for taking these items to finance her illegal departure from the country, which, by now, must have already been carried out.

Cairós was about to protest, pointing out the obvious absurdity of the claims he had just heard when El Big Mouth burst into the hallway, agitated and panting.

—The Jara house caught fire! —he shouted. —The transformer on the corner short-circuited, and it looks like sparks fell on the roof. The firefighters are already there.

The mustached man stood up and, as he headed for the exit, said in his apathetic voice,

—I'm done here, Sheriff Pérez. You can release Díaz.

Big Mouth took a moment to react, but finally, he found the key and opened the gate.

Cairós ran out of the station just in time to see another guy, with an equally intriguing appearance as the one who had interrogated him, walking quickly and getting into the car where the mustached man was waiting. The vehicle started and sped off a little too fast, leaving behind a cloud of dust in the night's commotion.

In the distance, the glow of the fire could be seen, and the shouts of firefighters battling the flames could be heard. El Big Mouth also stepped out of the station.

—Who are those guys? —Cairós asked.

—They're from the provincial capital...—the confused police officer replied with a shrug.

—I'm going to sleep, Big Mouth. If you want to arrest me again, you can find me at my house, —Cairós said as he walked away.

—I already told you, it's Sheriff Pérez.

Cairós slept poorly, with his sleep disturbed by vague nightmares. He woke up late, more tired than when he had gone to bed.

It was a cold day, with a gray sky threatening drizzle. The world seemed depressing and terribly empty.

He grabbed his jacket and went to the Jara house. Not much was left of the once majestic wooden structure. The firefighters had finished their work, and the place was deserted.

Carefully, the young man walked among the burnt debris until he reached where the library had been. To his surprise, the area was clear. Despite the fire and water, on the ground, around the mosaic with the Jara family coat of arms, the cryptic message that had sparked his concern remained indelible.

"How is it possible that it's still here?"

Cairós rubbed the sole of his shoe over one of the letters, but the character didn't fade in the slightest.

A gust of cold wind blew, forcing the young man to protect his hands in his jacket pockets. In one of them, his fingers found something unexpected.

He pulled out a small piece of paper, rolled up tightly. Carefully, he unrolled it.

Despite the madness that had overtaken her, Lucía's handwriting was unmistakable.

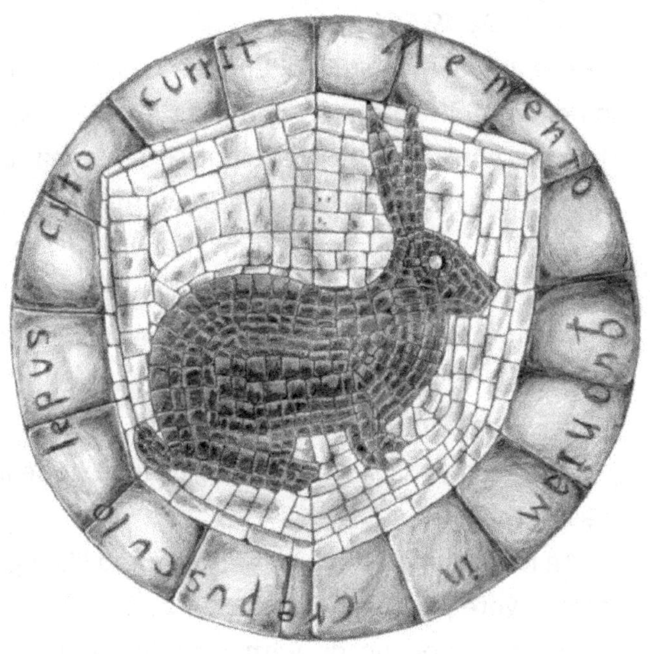

Since he was a child, he had noticed that the ceramic tile forming the hare's eye, instead of being square like the others, was hexagonal and much larger than the others. At the time, he hadn't paid much attention to that detail, but now...

"She must have slipped this in when she hugged me the last time."

The paper read:

"CHANCE

51 12 44 23 42 12 27

64 41 22 49 56"

The young man smiled. Chance was what Lucía called him in her most affectionate moments. She had explained to him that the word *kairós*, in ancient Greek, meant "the right or opportune moment," in other words, the chance to do something. Lucía had told him many times that, to her, he was her chance to be happy.

Without a doubt, the cryptic note was one of the riddles they used to solve for fun when they were kids, in that very place, sitting on that same mosaic.

Only that, back then, the strange indelible message wasn't there.

An idea flashed through Cairós' mind like lightning. Those letters were part of the puzzle.

"I have seven words, with a maximum of ten letters each, so..."

Slowly, he began decoding Lucía's message. In the end, the letters formed two words: "*Leporem oculo.*"

Cairós glanced around to make sure no one was watching him. There wasn't a soul in sight. He knelt on the mosaic and examined the coat of arms.

Since he was a child, he had noticed that the ceramic tile forming the hare's eye, instead of being square like the others, was hexagonal and much larger than the others. At the time, he hadn't paid much attention to that detail, but now...

The young man ran his finger over the different tile. It sank a few millimeters and returned to its normal level when Cairós removed his finger.

Almost instinctively, Cairós began pressing the ceramic piece to the rhythm of the traditional Jara family tune. A mechanism responded to the pressure, making the tile rise and fall. After seven presses, the hare's eye projected from the floor. It was a ten-centimeter-long hexagonal box.

Feverishly, Cairós activated the latch of the case, which opened with a click. Inside, there was a roll of paper and a small velvet pouch.

The young man unrolled the paper. In the unmistakable handwriting of his beloved Lucía, Cairós read:

"Chance, my love, I've found the opportunity to learn more about my family's past. I'm sure that in the halls of Carcosa, where all knowledge that has ever been and will ever be is kept, I can learn what I so desperately want to know. I've followed the clues, and I'm ready to walk the paths. I know you'll want to follow me, so I'm leaving you a seed of knowledge. I have no doubt that you, too, will find the way. I will love you forever, your Lucía."

Carefully, Cairós took out the contents of the velvet pouch. Hanging from a fine silver chain, a small teardrop-shaped stone swayed in the air. It had an incredibly polished surface, and embedded in the object, the young man saw a strange, oddly shaped, yellow symbol.

Cairós clenched the small stone tightly in his hand. Through clenched teeth, he swore under the ashen sky,

"I'm going to find you, Lucía, even if I must turn Creation upside down, I will find you. Wait for me, please!"

A few blocks away someone threw a cigarette butt out of the window of a parked car onto the wet street. Inside the vehicle an apathetic voice said.

—Another seed has been planted.

THE SERPENT´S TREASURE

On evenings like this, as I stroll along the beach in front of my hut, I let my memories fly like the seagulls and frigatebirds that stain the vast blue ocean with their white. These memories bring to mind, tormented by that horrifying being, the climax of the terrible adventure I once embarked upon through those distant mountains of madness.

After completing my routine of walking around the deserted islet where I have self-imposed exile due to the curse that deforms both my body and mind, I sit under the warm sun and let my thoughts drift beyond the fertile tobacco valleys, to the closed mountains that surround the dreadful cave where my curse was born. I repeatedly review the disastrous chain of events and torture myself, wondering what I could have done differently to prevent the whole affair from reaching such a tragic end.

As a medical doctor, graduated in the distant Spain, I diagnosed the rarest diseases and even managed to cure many of my patients from them. But I have never seen anything like the illness that is now corroding my own flesh.

I also dedicated much time to the study of zoology, my second great passion. Throughout my life, I have seen species of incalculable beauty and others of unspeakable ugliness. Yet, the image of that beast in the cave continues to gnaw at my nerves during these lonely nights.

I will only say that there are things that should have died thousands of years ago when humans were just learning to cover themselves with skins. That abomination was not an animal but a demon, the cause of the monstrous disease that disfigures me to this day.

As I may soon reach the end of my days, I am preparing to tell everything that happened. Perhaps my account will serve to prevent others from meeting a fate as disastrous as the one I bear.

Everything had begun with the Baron, known by that name due to his reserved and misanthropic personality, as no one knew his real name. In truth, the only thing known for certain was that he came from the Pyrenees region. Although the man undoubtedly had the bearing of someone with blue blood, his noble title was questioned.

The somber man had served in the Royal Navy of the Spanish Armada, holding positions in the Admiralty, but there was a rumor that he had also been part of pirate bands and even served as a captain of one.

I heard these claims from both townspeople and members of the high society of San Cristóbal de La Habana *vi lla*. I had never dignified such statements with any credit. However, it was undeniable that the man had a strange demeanor, bordering on the unpleasant.

The Baron lived on Aguiar Street, near the Plaza de la Catedral, in a dark baroque mansion. He often took long trips, leaving his butler alone in that gloomy place for weeks. The two were as gloomy as the house itself.

Sometimes, though, the Baron would stay locked up in his mansion for so long that he aroused the suspicion of the neighbors. They would see him arrive in his curtained carriage and, upon entering the mansion, he wouldn't come out for days. People would whisper that he always returned with loot from some plundered town, as he was supposedly a pirate. They claimed he had traveled through New Spain and worshipped the dead gods and beliefs of the Aztecs, that in his seclusion, he practiced witchcraft, and other such nonsense.

As a man of science, I, of course, didn't pay any attention to these dark tales. No gentleman in his right mind would give credence to such obscurantist gossip in the year 1789. Nevertheless, what happened afterward shattered many of my convictions.

I cling to the idea that everything I did was driven by the noble intention of saving Maria's life. I want to believe that my decision was a sane one.

Considering what I've already recounted, I will now tell you about the young woman who is the fulcrum of this entire story. A person diametrically opposed to the gloomy Baron.

Maria, a beautiful Creole maiden with honey-colored eyes, would wander the streets with a red handkerchief on her head, selling bouquets of flowers throughout the city. She was certainly shy, but she imbued everything around her with color and fragrance. I always greeted her in passing and often bought her lovely bouquets, tipping her with a kiss on the hand. Without a doubt, few things in La Habana were as pleasant as conversing with such a beautiful and simple lady. It was also heartwarming to see how she spoke with equal humility, whether to a beggar or a nobleman.

One day, during one of my routine walks, an unpleasant feeling overcame me as I passed by the Baron's mansion. I saw how the sinister individual, under the pretense of buying flowers, struck up a conversation with my young friend. It appeared to be a cordial conversation, the kind that Maria would offer to anyone, but that man exuded a malevolence I could somehow sense. A single glance was enough to convince me that none of his intentions toward my lovely friend were good. Thank heaven I followed that instinct, for if I had ignored my gut feeling, only God knows where sweet Maria's soul would be today.

The next afternoon, I saw my young friend, and as usual, she greeted me with a smile. After a brief chat, I didn't waste any time and, trusting in the confidence we had, I asked her about that encounter.

—Oh, you mean the Baron from Aguiar Street. Yes, he's someone who pays very well and even tips. I feel embarrassed to receive such attention. He's generous, but very serious. Did you see us talking?

—I happened to be passing by... You don't think I was spying on you, do you? —I looked at her playfully, and she smiled, blushing. After a brief silence, she said the Baron had kindly asked about her, to which she had naively answered all his questions, not suspecting his intentions. Things like her name, how many years she had lived here, and who her parents were, to which she replied that she had been an orphan since childhood. She mentioned that, upon hearing this, the Baron's eyes lit up, as if he had just been told the location of a chest full of gold.

When Maria, in turn, asked the nobleman his name, he evaded the question and, after offering another tip, politely took his leave.

Why the sinister Baron was so careful to conceal his identity, I didn't know, but I felt worried about his approach toward my innocent friend. It's not the behavior of a nobleman to inquire into a lady's personal past and details.

I said goodbye to Maria. She, with her usual joy, turned the corner, and there, among other carriages, was the Baron's carriage. Certainly, his dark-skinned driver had just parked the vehicle at his master's command to speak with the young lady. The eerie carriage, drawn by a purebred Arabian horse, seemed to swallow the daylight.

Startled and feeling the same unease as the first time, I approached the adjacent wall and carefully spied on the scene.

The supposed aristocrat leaned halfway out of the carriage. He wore a dark blue coat and a sailor's tricorn hat with a macaw feather. Maria spoke to him with her usual kindness. Stealthily, I overheard the sinister man, almost whispering.

—And are you going far?

—No, just to San Isidro, sir. Don't worry.

—Please, I insist. It's getting dark, and I'm sure you want to reach your home before nightfall.

There was something about him, something that reminded me of the stealth of a snake, perhaps his gaze or his manner of speaking. Whatever it was... nothing good could come of it.

—I insist, sir, and I appreciate your kindness, but as you can see, my basket is still full. It hasn't been a good day for sales. If you'll excuse me.

—In that case, let me propose a deal. I'll buy all the flowers, and you allow me to take you home. How does that sound?

—Are you serious? —Her golden eyes lit up with joy in the face of the Baron's serpent-like gaze. —I don't know what to say.

—You can start with a "yes, I accept". —They both laughed. She climbed into the carriage, helped by the hand of her buyer and escort.

—I truly don't know how to thank you.

I couldn't see her face, but I'm sure she was blushing from embarrassment at such a gesture of supposed kindness.

—Please, miss, —the hissing Baron said as Maria sat in the seat across from him. —Your company is thanks enough.

He closed the door and gave the order for the driver to depart. The carriage passed right in front of me. I lowered my head, pretending to check my pocket watch, but I didn't take my eyes off them.

Anyone would have sensed at least some alarm at the Baron's strange behavior. A man with a hidden life, taking a potential victim into his carriage, a young woman with no parents or anyone to defend her honor. It was a situation ripe for committing murder, rape, or any other atrocity without consequence.

My lack of action at that moment opened the door to the tragedy that befell us. If I had acted, I could have prevented the horrible events that followed and perhaps even avoided this unknown illness that promises me a fate worse than death. Today, I bitterly regret it.

After the carriage passed right in front of me, I felt a deep unease, knowing that María was inside. The young woman's crystal-clear voice was replaced by the obscene shouting of street vendors selling cheap goods and fruits, the shrill laughter of street children, and the clatter of horses' hooves on the road.

I barely noticed any of it. I felt overwhelmed by a drowsy guilt. The smell of fish and horse excrement seemed to accuse me, contrasting with the absent fragrance of María's black prince, carnations, and sunflowers.

Maybe it was all just my imagination. I was terribly judging a man I barely knew by sight. It was possible that the gentleman had no ill intentions, that he was even a good man, and the town gossip had only fed my suspicions. Thinking about these things, I told myself with resolve:

"If she doesn't show up tomorrow, I'll immediately go looking for her".

Believing this decision would ease my conscience, I returned home. But that night, I couldn't sleep. I had terrible nightmares in which I saw that unpleasant man physically abusing my friend while uttering praises in an unintelligible language. The figure was barely a silhouette with glowing eyes, but I knew it was him, with his shoulder-length hair, his tricorn hat adorned with a feather, reminiscent of bloodthirsty pirates like the Dutchman. But there was something else in the dreams, something I couldn't quite make out. Something like an immense boa appearing behind him, with glassy green eyes.

At this point, I woke up drenched in cold sweat. I couldn't take it anymore. I had to go find her. My conscience screamed at me, gripped by a terrible premonition. I had to know that María was safe. I couldn't, I shouldn't wait until the morning.

So, I prepared to go in search of the young woman. I armed myself with my flintlock pistol and a dagger. I knew roughly where my friend lived, so I walked down Compostela to Peña Pobre. I arrived at a dark opening and knocked on the door of a two-story house with a balustrade.

—Yes? —an old, wrinkled face with small eyes appeared through the rusty window of the door. —What do you want at this hour?

—Good night, and I'm sorry to have woken you. I need to know, if it's not too much trouble, if María, the young lady who sells flowers, lives here, —I tried to use my most polite tone in an attempt to soften the annoyance of waking this elderly woman in the middle of the night. But as I spoke, she responded with a kindness almost as great as her concern, without a trace of irritation or sleepiness.

—Oh, yes, sir! Of course! She's my granddaughter. She's lived with me since her parents died. I've raised her alone since she was very young, and she earns a living selling flowers all over San Cristóbal. She always returns before noon, and on slow sales days, she comes back by sunset. But today, look at the time, and she hasn't come home yet. I already went to the authorities, and they told me they'll start looking for her tomorrow. I can't sleep at all. Tell me... do you know anything?

At that moment, all my suspicions were confirmed. I was increasingly convinced of the Baron's wickedness. With my head spinning, my voice seemed to come out on its own.

—Oh, my God...

—Did something happen to my granddaughter? Do you know where she might be? Please tell me, good man, —I almost felt her starting to cry.

A deep sense of compassion toward the poor old woman overcame me. She deserved to know where her granddaughter was, but she wouldn't be able to bear the news of her abduction, so I told her a meager truth.

—Don't worry, I know where she might be. I promise that soon she'll be back here with you. She's a very dear friend of mine, and I won't let anything happen to her.

The old woman thanked me with tears in her eyes, and I set out to fulfill a promise I didn't know if I could keep. I wasn't even sure if María was still alive.

That's why my confident demeanor disappeared as soon as I turned the corner.

I was heading to the Baron's house, but my legs wouldn't obey me. I had no idea how to confront someone skilled with weapons, who had the audacity to abduct, like a real corsair, an innocent girl. God knows for what purpose.

I needed more information, so I went to a tavern where a good friend of mine was. He was a man who knew everyone and everything in the street. Without a doubt, a wise old fox of La Habana. Someone who, in my opinion, drank too much for being so religious and superstitious. Perhaps with him, I could find better information than the gossip from the rabble.

—José, my good friend, —he wasn't completely drunk yet when I saw him, —it's been a while since I've seen you, old dog!

—Doctor! —he almost fell off his chair when he saw me. I wasn't surprised at all to find him there, at such an ungodly hour—What brings you here?

I explained the situation, and when he heard me, he jumped and crossed himself.

—Jesus Christ, —he murmured, —I knew that guy wasn't right. Nobody knows his real name, not even me. What I do know is that he was a corvette captain and had several encounters with pirates. He retired after his ship was sunk. He used to travel frequently to Yucatán, and on his last trip, he took his wife and daughter. Why? That's a mystery. But they say he visited the Mayan ruins so much that he even learned their language, and God only knows what else. Rumor has it he worships Kukulkan and Quetzalcoatl... and since he never returned with his wife and daughter, people speculate that he sacrificed them at a dead temple in the jungle. Ah...—he shuddered, clutching a wooden rosary. —If what they say is true, I'd burn that sorcerer at the stake myself!

I was chilled by these rumors. In a low voice, I asked if he knew anything more, and he said that was all, except for some suspicions of piracy, that he might be the notorious Aragonés who captained a galleon called *Boa Negra*, looting the Dutch Caribbean. For me, everything was starting to make sense, and if most of it was true... then María was in danger!

—It's over. I'm going to find her right now! —I stood up from the chair without wasting any time, but José grabbed my arm, begging.

—Doctor... I beg you, don't go to that place alone. If you're going to help that poor soul, I... I'll go with you!

—Forgive me, José. I know you've always looked out for my safety, but I can't put someone else at risk. I must face this alone. I'm armed, —and I showed him my firearm. —Don't worry. Thank you for everything.

I thought I had convinced him to give up when he saw the handle of the pistol on my belt. When I left the tavern, his voice made me turn around.

—Doctor! —He looked at me as if I were a lamb being led to slaughter. —May God protect you.

—So be it, my friend, —I replied with a smile, trying to ease his worry.

I crossed the dark streets of the city, chilled to the bone and accompanied by a hissing wind, like a snake. The windows of the colonial houses seemed like empty eyes, pitying me, gazing with indescribable compassion.

The cold autumn night air carried faint sounds, the distant passing of a carriage, the laughter of a courting couple in the darkness, a groaning beggar snoring in a doorway, my increasingly labored breathing, the sound of my boots on the cobblestones getting closer, and closer, and closer...

Finally, I arrived at the sinister house. I stood before it, barely feeling my shallow breathing. It didn't matter if I was afraid. The only thing that mattered at that moment was her. I made sure my gun was within reach, and before I even realized how, I was inside the Baron's mansion.

The dark interior of the mansion made it difficult to distinguish the details of the place. A figure took advantage of the shadows and lunged at me.

Was my attacker the sinister Baron? No. After struggling with the assailant, I realized that my opponent was the butler, a man who, despite his advanced age, demonstrated tremendous strength and agility.

In a few swift moves, the butler had me pinned to the ground. He pulled something sharp from his nightshirt. Sweating cold with fear, I tried to grip his hand tightly so he wouldn't stab me. The blade was almost touching my chest when I heard the sound of breaking glass behind the attacker.

The old man was momentarily stunned and fell unconscious from the blow of a bottle delivered by a saving hand.

—Damned criminal! I don't blame him for defending the house... But if I hadn't come sooner, you'd be at St. Peter's gate by now. Are you alright, doctor?

—José! —I had never felt so terrified and happy in the same minute. My good friend had apparently downed two more mugs of rum to muster the courage to follow me. —I can't believe you're here. I should scold you for coming after me... But you saved my life! —I think I nearly cried with joy when I saw his scruffy face in the darkness as he extended a hand to help me up.

—Sorry, my code of honor doesn't allow me to leave a comrade in danger. Let's tie up this scoundrel. He probably has information about his master's whereabouts.

My eyes widened. My ears throbbed with a splitting headache, and I felt a tightness in my chest, as if the butler had truly stabbed me. The Baron wasn't in his mansion, and neither was María. He had taken her. God knows where or for what. I felt that all hope of finding her had vanished... except for the information the Baron's servant might provide.

We sat the unconscious butler in a chair and tied him up. José tried to rouse him. I lit a candle I found in the room. In its flickering light, I took in as much of the room's decor as I could.

The space was medium-sized, with high walls that reached a red-tiled ceiling. It looked like a study, with a dusty bookshelf containing books alternating with jars of animals preserved in formaldehyde. A heavy mahogany desk dominated the room, its drawers locked with padlocks. On the desk, a jade inkwell in the shape of a dragon's or feathered serpent's head caught my eye, along with strange idols of Mayan appearance. A giant stuffed boa hung from the ceiling, almost causing me to scream. The floor was adorned with a jaguar-skin rug.

And there, on the wall, in a pine-framed painting inlaid with obsidian, was a familiar canvas. The image depicted a young mestiza girl with large golden eyes, a native-looking woman, and the unmistakable Baron. His viper-like eyes seemed to glare at me cruelly through the painting. It was the first time I saw so clearly the sharp features of that sinister man.

Noticing that the servant was beginning to wake, José slapped him to bring him fully to his senses. The butler turned his face but didn't utter a word.

—Ah, you're awake, you scoundrel. Were you going to kill the doctor like a dog, weren't you, you rogue?

—My master gave me orders to protect his home, even using force against intruders.

The man spoke with a coldness that scared me. He didn't seem to care about being tied up by us. He was merely a loyal lackey. I began to question him.

—A young woman who sells flowers throughout the city. María. You probably don't know her name, but I saw her with "your master", getting into his carriage this afternoon. She's been missing since then. What do you know about that?

—Absolutely nothing, except that my master usually takes young women home out of good faith, —he spoke with the same indifference, as if a mere dog's life was at stake.

—Good faith? —my friend said, his blood hotter than mine. —Listen, you wretched servant, we know what the Baron is up to, and it's nothing good. That innocent girl's life is in danger...

—I repeat that I don't know what you're talking about, sir, —he said pompously, daring to interrupt José, who turned red with rage.

—Oh, really?! —he clenched his fists, restraining himself from punching the butler.

Certainly, it wasn't wise to anger a man like him, but the servant remained expressionless. José turned to me.

—In that case, doctor, I have something to show you that I found when we entered.

I almost fainted at the sight of the object. It was the handkerchief María wore on her head! It even had the same perfume. My friend had been here against her will! Unable to contain myself, I drew my pistol from my belt, my hand trembling, unable to bear the sight of that bootlicker's face, who, with the same dryness and cynicism, said:

—I'm sorry. I have no idea who that belongs to.

—Speak, you, miserable dog! —my friend shouted, with the same fury he had infected me with. —Where is she?!

Then I noticed something I hadn't seen before, something that truly made my skin crawl. Among the various sculptures representing ancient Mayan gods resting on the desk, the effigy of the god Kukulkan, the Feathered Serpent, stood out. All the figures surrounded a carved circle in the wood, bordered by strange hieroglyphs, with a zigzagging symbol in the center of the circumference.

José approached as well and couldn't hide the horror he felt upon seeing what lay at the foot of the enigmatic statue.

—My God!

The image of Kukulkan stood about nine or ten inches tall, carved from a very dark stone. Its head faced forward, and its eyes were made of rubies, giving the image an immense touch of malevolence. At the feet of the idol were white candles, worn down, along with python skins and dead hummingbirds. A truly profane and horrible sight.

We snapped out of our shock when the bound butler began to laugh sardonically under his breath. His entire demeanor of being emotionally dead gave way to a kind of hysterical madness when he realized he had been exposed.

I aimed my gun at him again. It was becoming increasingly clear that the rumors surrounding the Baron were true and that this man was his accomplice. I had to make him talk. I told him I knew about his master's exploits in the jungles of Yucatán, that I was aware of his religious worship, pointing to the evidence on the desk, to which he laughed even more hysterically and said:

—Yes, it's all true. My master worships the Feathered Serpent... the great Kukulkan, Lord of Life. The mighty Quetzalcoatl promised my master power over the winds and rains... I will go with him too... Oh, great Yig, Father of the Serpents!

—Tell me where he took her, bloody madman!

—He will go to his dwelling, in the mountains where the sun sets... He will go to the cave where his crew's treasure is kept... They already have the Taíno girl, and my master has the virgin... The offering for the mighty Kukulkan.

There was no longer any doubt. All the evidence pointed to the fact that the Baron was indeed a deranged practitioner of religions that the conquistadors had tried to eradicate. And if the sacrifice was true... My God, I couldn't just stand by and do nothing. This time, José spoke up.

—What happened to the Baron's wife and daughter?

But the man didn't answer anymore. He had become a mindless shell, raving about Kukulkan and Yig. He warned, between praises, about the curse that would fall on anyone who killed one of their children. All while convulsing with laughter. Laughter that echoed throughout the eerie silence of the house.

We realized, terrified, that he and the Baron were the only inhabitants of the mansion. There was no one else, no servants, no slaves. Just the two of us and this madman.

The first light of dawn announced the start of a new day. My friend's voice broke the silence.

—Let's go. This man is completely insane. He'll burn in hell. The house he mentioned... I've heard about it. I know where it is. It's in a valley between the mountains, in the region where the settlers grow tobacco, more than twenty leagues from here.

José, in a gesture of pity, untied the madman. But the old man, in a fit of fury, lunged at us like a wild beast, trying to kill us. More out of fear than conscious intent, I pulled the trigger, and my pistol fired.

When I checked the fallen butler, I found that the bullet had pierced his heart. He was dead. I must confess that despite being a doctor, I didn't feel any sympathy for him. All I felt was rage at his complicity with his maniacal master. José, much more compassionate than I, closed the man's eyes and whispered a prayer.

We immediately left that cursed house. A few hours later, the two of us were far from the city, frantically driving a carriage down dirt roads, heading for that unknown place. I had no idea what we would face there. I pray that Almighty

God will one day grant me the blessing of forgetting the abomination I had the misfortune to witness in those lands.

After three days, we had covered most of the ominous journey. According to José, we had only about five leagues left to travel.

My friend was well-trained in arms and hunting, for which he had bought a robust Alano dog that accompanied us on this adventure. As for me, I had Caronte, my excellent Saint Hubert tracking dog.

Our carriage, pulled by a pair of Andalusian horses, traveled through beautiful valleys and hills that, despite it being autumn, still displayed a precious greenery. We saw few farms along the way, and at one of them, we had to replace a damaged wheel due to the roughness of the road. We took the opportunity to ask if anyone had seen the Baron's carriage pass by.

We received chilling information.

The overseer, a sturdy but polite *criollo* who had recently arrived from the *villa* of Trinidad, informed us that the day before, a black curtained carriage drawn by the blackest purebred Arabian horse he had ever seen passed through. It was driven by a gentleman wearing a tricorn hat adorned with a feather, who had approached to ask for water for his horse.

The good man couldn't provide more details about the driver of the dark carriage, as he had only been working on the farm for a short time and wasn't familiar with the local settlers. The mysterious gentleman had neither given his name nor said where he was headed or where he had come from. However, the overseer casually mentioned that while he was carrying the buckets to water the horse, he had caught a glimpse of a girl asleep inside the carriage.

I was stunned.

We knew very well that this was the deranged Baron. The girl in the carriage could be none other than the poor María. She was probably more unconscious than asleep, so that the damned man could control her at his will.

We thanked him for the information and left immediately.

The *villa* of San Cristóbal de La Habana was now far to the east. The passage of noble carriages, the clamor of the street vendors, and the usual chatter of the city had been replaced by the murmur of the wind through the *caguairán* and mahogany trees, the whistles of *cateyes* and *pitirres* from the palm trees, and the pleasant sound of a mountain stream where we stopped to water the animals.

On the last day of the journey, we saw no more signs of human life in the region. The endless plains, sporadically adorned with gentle mogotes, gradually turned into difficult terrain. Sometimes the hills were so steep that we had to push the carriage along the narrow forest paths. The picturesque Creole tobacco colonies were left behind, the last bastions of civilization. Ahead of us lay the enigmatic depths of the mountains where Indians and runaway slaves hid.

Nightfall overtook us in a forested area so dense that we could barely see the trail we were following. It was then that we heard the faint sound of a mayohuacán drum, accompanied by maracas and shouting. We realized we were near a Taíno village, one of the few remaining indigenous settlements in the most remote parts of the island. We decided it would be a good place to spend the night.

The village was in a forest clearing, bordered by stone slabs embedded in the ground. It consisted of several *caneyes* surrounding a circle where all the inhabitants were dancing frenetically to the crazed rhythm of their *areíto*. The chief, who introduced himself courteously as Caimancaona, spoke perfect Spanish.

—Welcome to our community. If you wish to spend the night, we will host you without issue, though I can't guarantee you'll get much sleep.

We accepted the invitation, and after a bath in a nearby stream, we ate a meal of roasted *jutía* and *cazabe* with the village's great *behíque* (shaman). José, always more daring than I, didn't hesitate to ask,

—And what is the reason for such a celebration here?

—There is no celebration today, —the old *behíque* told us. —We are driving away evil spirits. Currently, the great *majá* of the caves is furious. We are trying to calm its anger with the mayohuacán. It has always been this way. But this time, some men from the sea took a young woman from the village. They took her to the cave of the *majá* to offer her as a sacrifice so that the monster will sleep through the winter.

At that moment, I remembered what the crazed servant had said about the Baron's crew. —They already have the Taíno girl, —he had confessed before completely losing his sanity.

Was there a horrifying connection between the Indians' myths about a colossal *majá* in a cave in the mountains and the Baron's cult and his infamous buccaneers, who worshipped Kukulkan, a serpent-shaped god adored by the Mayans, said to bring the rains and the wind?

During one of the Baron's eerie trips to Yucatán, his wife and daughter never returned, leading to suspicions of a horrible sacrifice to that deity. Nevertheless, a terrible name came to my mind, the name of a mythical god the butler had mentioned and perhaps the indigenous people knew.

—Great *behíque*... do you know a god called... Yig?

—Close your mouth, fool! —the elderly *behíque* stood up at once, pointing his trembling hand at me. —Do not speak the name of the Father *Majá*. Follow me.

The old shaman led us through the dance to a secluded place beyond the stone slabs. It was a small hut surrounded by ropes adorned with protective beads to ward off evil spirits.

The shaman explained that the beads were not meant to keep the bad spirits out... but rather to keep them well contained inside.

The hut was dimly lit. The flames of some torches on the walls cast a chaotic dance of light and shadows. The floor was covered with a thick layer of straw. Behind some wooden bars, we saw a young Indian man sleeping naked.

The old man spoke in a very low voice, so as not to wake him...

—He is Yayamaturey. He dared to kill one of Yig's sacred *majás*. The skin of the beast is in my house. It can wrap around the trunk of a palm tree. The curse has fallen upon him... now he will become one of Yig's children

Understanding that the indigenous pandemonium wouldn't let us sleep, we decided to leave the Taíno village. Once we were far enough away that the insane sound of the drums was nothing more than a distant murmur, we camped next to a fire and decided to spend the night there. The good Indians had left us a generous supply of food and some of their primitive protective amulets.

After a light dinner, we prepared to sleep, but I couldn't fall asleep. Sensing my insomnia, José turned to me.

—You can't sleep, I know. Neither can I. Not after seeing that man in the hut. God, doctor... he was turning into a *majá*.

—Of course not, —my mind tried to explain what I had glimpsed under the light of the torches. Perhaps it was my disturbed imagination, but I could swear his skin seemed... scaly. —It's likely a severe case of ichthyosis. It's a congenital disease that...

—With all due respect, doctor, I don't know much about medicine, but the shaman said he got sick after killing the *majá*. It wasn't a congenital disease. Besides, does that illness make your hair fall out?

—Yes. It also causes the skin to look like that, preventing sweating. It makes the eyes dry up like those of a lizard. Unfortunately, there's no cure. But I understand your point. The young man didn't contract the syndrome from birth. Maybe...

—You should have examined him despite the old *behíque* 's protests. I still think something terrible is hiding in these hills. Did you see the size of that skin the shaman had in his hut?

He was referring to an immense snakeskin hanging in a hidden section of the *bohío*. It was grayish in color and looked quite thick. From the position of the scales, I could see it was just a section of the body. Its size must have been colossal, measuring three to four feet wide. It was undoubtedly a true anaconda.

It must have been an admirable feat for the young Yayamaturey to have hunted such a specimen. However, he had been exiled from his own village under the supposed curse of Yig, with a rare illness that, in my medical opinion, was a mutation of ichthyosis.

Nevertheless, in my capacity as a zoologist, I had never seen evidence of such a colossal snake on the entire island. The largest specimens I observed were in the Amazon jungle, thousands of leagues to the south.

Perhaps, in a remote time when Cuba was connected to Yucatán, some specimens had managed to migrate through the jungle and settled there. But even that was doubtful since no such large serpents had been discovered in this region. Yet the evidence was there before our eyes. Evidence of a creature that could have crushed all our bones with a single squeeze.

The settlers had a legend about the Mother of Waters, a mythological being who, they said, would never let the river or lagoon where it swam dry up. But... could what we had seen be the remains of that fantastic creature?

—Ah... good night, doctor. They say the early bird catches the worm, and we must catch a very nasty fat worm. See you tomorrow, —José said, yawning and turning over in his blanket.

Lying in my improvised bed, I thought about the story Chief Caimancaona had told us before we left.

According to him, many years ago, the god Huracán had struck the region with unprecedented intensity, leaving behind destruction like never before. Then, from the east came a white man. He arrived peacefully and helped the Indians rebuild their *bohíos* and *conucos*.

The white man lived with the Indians for a long time, showing them how to hunt hutias and deer more effectively using firearms and teaching them his language. It didn't take long for him to marry one of the women of the village. Before long, they had a beautiful daughter with golden eyes named Iyali.

The stranger built a large house in a nearby valley and went to live there with his new family, although the little girl enjoyed visiting the village.

Time passed, and the little girl grew into a beautiful young woman. It was no surprise when a love blossomed between her and Yayamaturey, the strongest warrior in the tribe. They seemed more like deities from legends than mere humans.

The real surprise came when the girl's parents fiercely opposed the young love. They forbade the girl from returning to the village and made it clear to Yayamaturey that he was not welcome near their house in the valley.

Iyali, like any passionate teenager, disobeyed her parents, sneaking out many times to see her beloved. She told him strange things about her parents, who said she had to remain pure for a long journey, at the end of which she would present herself to what her mother referred to as "Him."

The girl suspected something very sinister. When her parents locked themselves in the mansion's attic, offering prayers and praises to an unknown god named Yig, or Kukulkan, it gave her chills.

Fearing that his beloved's own parents might harm her, Yayamaturey secretly visited her room every day. All their tension and fear culminated in an abject event that left the young Indian perplexed.

One day, Yayamaturey descended from the hills to visit the girl as usual. The infinite horror and dismay he experienced when he found the valley house completely abandoned were overwhelming. Violating the prohibition to approach the place, he entered and searched every room. His heart shattered when he found a note hidden in a secret spot where his beloved Iyali kept the things she treasured most.

"My dearest Yaya,

If you're reading this, I'm sorry. By now, I'll be far away or maybe even dead. I tried to escape, but they locked me in the bedroom.

I've discovered everything, everything they plan to do with me.

They want to take me to a temple in the jungle, beyond the sea, to sacrifice me to 'Him.'

That man, whom I refuse to call father, is a selfish monster who uses my mother for his own ends. Her love for him has blinded her completely, and she will sacrifice herself as well. She cares neither for her life nor mine.

Even if you never see me again, I want you to know that I'll love you forever from beyond, and our love, unknown to them, will be our revenge.

Forever yours... Iyali."

And so, it was. Yayamaturey never saw Iyali again. Maddened by anger and grief, he armed himself with weapons and provisions and set out westward, toward the land of the ancestors. He was determined to follow his beloved's trail. He returned later with the huge piece of *majá* skin we saw at the shaman's house.

In his frenzy, the young man had killed one of Yig's *majás* , the serpent god that the tribe's ancestors, who had come from the Mayan jungles long ago, had known in distant lands. The curse fell upon him. The relentless punishment for ending the life of the feared *majá*.

Lying under the moonlight, I meditated. Next to me, José's snores accompanied those of the dogs. It was clearer than water that the white man who had helped the Indians was none other than the vile Baron. That demon had married one of the Taíno women to have her bear a child. Without a doubt, they were the women in the painting at the mansion on Aguiar Street.

Obviously, his intention wasn't to have a family life. To him, those people were nothing more than offerings to be sacrificed to Yig. He seduced the Taíno woman to the point of folly, and after she gave birth to Iyali, they had the innocent soul for the sacrilegious ritual. But something had gone wrong, and now he was trying again.

Iyali mentioned in her letter that her romance with the Taíno would be her revenge. What did she mean by that? It was that, to perform the ceremony, they needed the soul of a Taíno woman and that of a virgin. Everything indicated that Iyali was no longer a virgin because of her romance with Yayamaturey, a key piece in foiling the wretched Baron's plans. Undoubtedly, an epic revenge against her abhorrent father.

Thus, the defeated Baron had returned to his home in La Habana and was now trying again with the poor María and the kidnapped native woman from the village.

I didn't want to think about anything else at that moment. The day had been exhausting, and I was already pondering the next day. Many doubts and ideas swirled in my mind. The Baron, the pirates, Yig, the Mayans... María. All of it condensed into a terrible nightmare I experienced while wrapped in the wild breeze of the forest.

In my dreams, I entered a sinister cave with an underground lake. At the bottom, I saw heaps of gold under the water. There, coiled over the treasure, a massive *majá* slithered slowly. I dreamed of María, in the hands of the Aragonés, being taken to jungles once inhabited by the great Mayan civilization.

I dreamed I stood atop an immense stepped pyramid under a violent storm. On the stone altar, a young woman was being stabbed by the Baron, who was pulling out her heart as an offering to Kukulkan, the feathered serpent. The executioner rhythmically chanted the victim's name: Iyali! Iyali! But the face of the sacrificed body was that of my María.

I felt transported to a time long past, under the muted sound of drums and flutes, perhaps thousands of years before the Spanish arrived there. I saw how the Day and the Night, Quetzalcoatl and Tezcatlipoca, the one with the black mirror, clashed in a hand-to-hand battle under the cold gaze of Metztli, at the dawn of time.

Before I descended further into the madness of the dream, José woke me. The day had just begun to break.

—Doctor, wake up. Come on, we're almost there. You're sweating. Did you have nightmares again?

I washed my face, and after breakfast, we resumed our journey.

Sometime later, we stopped at the top of a hill from which we could see a valley densely populated with fruit trees. In the center, there was a small cluster of colonial wooden and tile buildings.

—We've arrived. This is the Baron's summer mansion.

At that moment, the forest, teeming with birdsong and moist with the morning dew, stopped being something beautiful and peaceful to me. The Baron's influence transformed that beautiful place into something evil and unsettling. I felt a shiver as I spotted a sinister figure among the buildings.

—Hurry, José, give me the spyglass!

Through the object, I saw an enlarged image of the cursed man. He was in front of the stable adjacent to the house, saddling his black horse. My friend snatched the spyglass from my hands.

—By the devil... it's him. We must catch him!

We jumped from our carriage like lightning and unhitched the horses as quickly as possible. There was no time to saddle them, or the scoundrel would escape. We released the dogs and started the chase, pistols in hand, racing down the steep path. We were still far away when the villain noticed our presence and the noisy dogs. He mounted his steed and fled toward the hills on the other side of the valley. Even so, I fired a desperate shot to stop him. My shot had no effect.

—Scum from hell! He's running into the hills like a cowardly *jutía*!

—We must check the house! They could be there! —I said, turning the horse by the mane.

I wish we had never stopped to search for anything there. Not only because it was a complete waste of time, but because what we found in the attic was something I'll never forget.

We searched the house from top to bottom, even the basement, finding nothing particularly strange. It looked like a typical house in the region, with red tiles, double-leaf doors and windows, mahogany furniture, and hunting trophies like hutias, deer, and macaws.

Unfortunately, there was no sign of María.

But there was one place left to search, up there, where the wall met the ceiling. The silent attic.

We expected to find my friend and maybe the poor Indian girl, tied up and gagged, begging to be freed. Heaven help us, why wasn't that the case? What we found there was much worse.

That accursed attic, smelling of dust and an open grave, held, on a small shelf, a book I should never have touched. The volume had black leather covers with iron studs. Our curiosity led us to open it and glimpse its sacrilegious contents.

I don't dare mention its name. It was enough to leaf through it briefly to be horrified to the core. The most macabre thing was reading the sections marked by the Baron himself. The abominable lines, written in archaic characters, made me understand the deranged nature of the cult that the vile demon wanted to carry out.

The cursed text spoke of the favors that the Serpent God granted to those who made pacts with him. To the Aztecs, he was Quetzalcoatl, and to the Mayans, Kukulkan, but his name had always been Yig, bearer of a curse that would befall anyone who killed his children.

The Taínos of that region had known him since the arrival of their ancestors, back in the time when Europe was learning to forge bronze. He presented himself peacefully to the natives. But for some reason, he would enter a frenzy in the fall and had to be appeased.

The great Yig also offered his followers powers over the rains and tremendous longevity in exchange for the blood of a young Taíno woman of Mesoamerican origin and that of a virgin. The pact would be sealed when one of Yig's *majás* devoured the offerings alive.

As macabre evidence that the demon in human form had already attempted the vile ritual, we found two skulls on a kind of stone altar. Under each of them was a label. "Dear Ixchel." "My beloved daughter Iyali." They were the skulls of the Baron's wife and daughter! The vile Aragonés had sacrificed them! But, due to Iyali's love for Yayamaturey, he had failed in his endeavor.

Now, he was trying again, replacing his wife with the Taíno woman and his innocent daughter with my poor friend María!

We left that profane place deeply disturbed.

After clearing our heads in the fresh morning air, we focused on the hunt. It was time to capture that infamous man.

I gave Caronte the red handkerchief I had carefully kept with me. I was well aware of the St. Hubert dog's brilliant gift for tracking people over more than ten miles. The Alano would make up for the older dog's age with his intimidating strength.

We already knew the Baron's terrible plans. We just needed to find him with our dogs and drag him before justice for charges of witchcraft, piracy, and murder, thus bringing him to the gallows. The vile Aragonés, the Baron of Aguiar Street, was indeed a filthy sorcerer.

We were very close now, galloping like lightning behind the dogs that led the way. Our enraged and eager hearts beat in rhythm with the horses' hooves on the ground. Until finally, we reached the mouth of a cave so sinister that even the two dogs hesitated.

It looked like the mouth of a demon. The stalactites inside simulated fierce fangs. It was lined with vines hanging over the entrance, and despite being in a densely forested area, no bird could be heard singing. There was the pirate's horse.

My faithful Caronte hadn't failed us. María was inside, deep in the cave.

Neither weapons nor dogs nor the combined courage of José and I prepared us for what we would see in that place, led by the dogs. Something that, in my judgment, confirmed everything written in the vile book we had found in the attic.

After a tedious walk through the dark interior of the cave, nervous from my friend's constant prayers, we reached a five-foot drop over a circle illuminated by torches stuck into the grotesque rock columns reaching the high ceiling. In the chamber, there was a lagoon next to which twenty ragged men moved. There was no doubt that this mob was the Aragonés' crew, and all indications were that they would participate in the ritual.

In the center of the cave was the Baron. The Aragonés. The devotee of a belief long thought eradicated by the conquistadors.

Naked from the waist up, the evil man had his torso painted with red and black stripes. He wore jade earrings and necklaces like the high priests of the dead Chichen Itzá. He chanted to Yig in Spanish and Mayan.

There, finally, I saw the object of this mad adventure. I had been searching for her with my eyes until I saw her, tied behind a wide rock facing the lagoon. There, next to the poor Taíno woman, lay her.

—María! —I couldn't help it. I screamed with all my might, interrupting the unholy ritual.

All the desperation and rage of the past few days were released in a single name, in a single word... María. Did I love her? Yes... of course, I loved her! I was determined to protect her at all costs! I had embarked on this terrible journey with my friend... just for her, to finally see her free from the clutches of the loathsome pirate-sorcerer!

We jumped from the ledge with loaded pistols and sabers in hand. Our shouts and those of the horde of buccaneers charging toward us echoed like cannons in the spectral cave, scattering countless bats.

The ratio of men to men was ten to one, but my friend and I knew how to handle our sabers with skill. It didn't matter how many there were. We would end the miserable lives of anyone who stood between me and my beloved María, her guardian angel. We would massacre any demonic pirate.

I managed to take down two with my pistol shots. José killed three. With no time to reload, we engaged in hand-to-hand combat with our sabers.

Although they had no firearms, the pirates seemed quite confident fighting there, in the bowels of the earth. Their captain continued his ceremony as if nothing had happened, which seemed to encourage them. We clashed in duels, our blades colliding.

The powerful Alano dog did his part, attacking the groins of some of the ruffians until they were out of the fight. Caronte, for his part, barked from a corner, urging us not to surrender to these savages.

For a moment, I was distracted when I saw the Baron, half-naked, next to María. She begged me with tear-filled eyes to save her. One of the pirates took advantage of the opportunity and raised his saber against me. I didn't have time to lift my sword to block the attack, but José's blade emerged, triumphant, piercing the pirate's chest, killing him instantly.

—Go to save the women, doctor! I'll handle these cursed ruffians! —my friend shouted.

I looked around, and only a few men remained. The fierceness and skill with which José fought were extremely impressive. I didn't want to leave him alone, but now María's life was in greater danger than ever.

Weapons in hand, I headed toward the epicenter of the infernal ceremony, determined to save her. A demonic laugh from the Baron stopped me in my tracks. The vile man chanted between maniacal laughter.

—Reveal yourself, O Great Yig´s Son! Come, guardian of the heaps of gold! Come to receive your pure offering and make a pact with your servant! Grant me power over the hurricanes for many years to come, I, the Baron! Grant me power to plunder more gold and bring it to you, Offspring of Yig! Rise, Mother of the Waters of the Grotto!

From the men still fighting for the Aragonés to José, from the two tied-up women to me, and even our fierce dogs, we all trembled with terror in that bat-filled grotto when, after a rumbling sound from the water in the lagoon, the inconceivable appeared...

A colossal gray serpent, with a head nearly two feet wide and milky-white eyes, emerged from the water. Its deformed mouth was filled with countless needle-like, drooling teeth. This creature was a species never before seen by Science. It was a horrifying Mother of Waters, just like the one that had appeared in my dreams.

A wave of terror swept through the entire cavern. The Baron's men fell into a hypnotic trance. José and I lowered our weapons, crushed by an ancient, primal horror. Even our loyal dogs lay flat on their bellies, ears down, whimpering.

The first of us to react was my faithful Caronte, who overcame his fear and barked with an indomitable air of defiance. José shook off the paralysis, as if breaking a spell that had been cast over him, and attacked the pirates still standing, finishing them off.

My terror paralysis ended when I saw the giant creature moving its head toward María and the Indian woman, who were screaming through their gags and writhing in their bindings.

The Baron seemed to be in a trance, swaying in sync with the serpent, his eyes closed, mimicking the monster's movements.

I shakily loaded a pistol, trying to figure out how to deliver an effective shot to such an animal. Its skull was likely too hard. The mouth wasn't in my line of fire... Good heavens, the beast's massive, forked tongue was already brushing the Taíno woman!

—Doctor! —José's voice reached me like a dying echo from a terrible dream. —Aim for the eyes... the eyes!

More than advice, it was a revelation to me. I raised my hand and aimed at the milky eye of the *majá*.

The bullet pierced its brain.

The monster hissed and convulsed in pain, emitting shrieks that chilled the soul under the yellowish torchlight. The Baron screamed and fell to the side, clutching his eye, as if he had been the one shot.

The colossal beast's head slumped by the shore, almost at María's feet, who fainted on the spot. The weight of the creature's body dragged its dead head into the depths of the cold lagoon, extinguishing that horror once and for all.

The Baron staggered to his feet, as if blown by the wind. His eye bled profusely, inexplicably. He began walking toward me.

I had no bullets left. I threw my pistol to the ground and gripped my sword with renewed strength. I advanced toward the Baron.

When our eyes met, I could feel the rage between us. In his black eyes, I saw hatred for me, for frustrating his monstrous plans, for relentlessly pursuing him without giving him a moment's rest.

As for me, I would never forgive him for kidnapping my beloved María.

The fight wasn't over. It had just begun.

The Alano dog leapt from the side onto the malevolent pirate-sorcerer, knocking him down with his massive body, trying to bite him. But the Baron managed to position his sword under the dog's neck and slit its throat with a precise and fierce cut.

I shakily loaded a pistol, trying to figure out how to deliver an effective shot to such an animal. Its skull was likely too hard. The mouth wasn't in my line of fire... Good heavens, the beast's massive, forked tongue was already brushing the Taíno woman!

Before the cursed man could get back on his feet, I charged at him with the intention of slashing him to pieces. But the crafty villain had an excellent defense, even from the ground.

The exhaustion from my previous battle began to take its toll. My body felt heavy, and my muscles weren't moving with the same speed and flexibility. The Baron, taking advantage of this, began to overpower me with each attack.

Suddenly, with a skillful trip, the diabolical man knocked me down. The impact with the ground left me breathless for a moment.

My opponent seized the opportunity. He jumped on top of me with his sword ready. I barely managed to raise my weapon to block the deadly strike.

Our roles had reversed. He was on top of me, his blade aimed at my chest. I was blocking his fatal thrust with my sword, trying to fend him off with all the strength I had left.

I thought I was going to collapse. Slowly, I was giving in to the Baron's prodigious strength. I believed I would never see María again. I glanced at her and, in farewell, closed my eyes.

I heard a thunderous sound echoing through the cave. The incredible pressure on me suddenly eased.

When I opened my eyes, the Baron's arms hung limp, and he looked at me, stunned.

—You... you've killed him. Yig has said it. 'Cursed will be forever the one who kills one of my children.' My death is sweeter than the fate that awaits you.

Those were the last words that vile demon uttered before collapsing on top of me. With a shove, I pushed the disgusting body off and ran to where my friend was kneeling, his pistol still smoking in his hand.

José's well-aimed shot had saved my life once again.

—I'll never be able to thank you enough! Three times... three times you've saved my life! You're a friend worth more than gold.

—Third time's the charm, —I noticed a certain melancholy in his expression, in his gaze, and in the way he said the phrase. —Safe travels back...

That was when he collapsed, and I saw a sword wound that had pierced his torso. I did everything I could to save him, but I didn't have time to stop his already advanced internal bleeding.

José died in my arms.

I wept bitterly for the loss of my great companion. It was unfair that he had saved my life three times, and I couldn't save his even once. The best tribute I could offer him at that moment was a small burial with stones, leaving his sword plunged into the earth where my friend José would rest forever. Next to him, I buried the brave Alano, who had also given his life in that unequal struggle.

María and the young Indian woman, now recovered from their mortal fear, prayed with me and laid flowers on the graves of their saviors.

On our way back to La Habana, we returned the young Taíno woman to her village. I felt honored to see how, through tears of joy, they celebrated her return, offering us gifts, fruits, and expressions of gratitude. For obvious reasons, we agreed to omit the part of the story in which I killed the great *majá*.

When we arrived in the city, I fulfilled my promise of reuniting María with her grandmother.

The kind old woman was already dressed in mourning because my promise had taken more than a painful week. You can imagine the immense joy she felt at seeing her beloved granddaughter again.

As for María and me, we had a short courtship. But we couldn't marry because my illness forced me to distance myself from everything and everyone.

Yes, today I find myself far from home, living with my faithful Caronte under the roof of a cabin on a secluded key in the middle of the sea, away from her so that she won't see me in this horrible condition. I have the same illness as Yayamaturey.

Ichthyosis is nothing compared to this.

My skin has turned scaly and a greenish-gray, and a membrane has formed over my eyes. All my hair has fallen out, my tongue has begun to split, and I feel numb in winter due to the cooling of my blood.

I am starting to detect heat through my increasingly blind eyes. My intellect diminishes with each passing day, and I fear the moment will come when I am nothing more than a series of primitive instincts.

To hell with all my knowledge of the sciences that try to explain the inexplicable.

The Baron's last words were true! Just like the Indian Yayamaturey, I am becoming a Son of Yig!

The activity level of a snake is determined by the temperature of the air. That is why, in this winter of 1789 of our Lord, before falling prey to a long hibernation, I have sworn by all the gods that when I wake, if I still possess my mind and limbs, I will leave this islet.

There, in the abandoned house in the valley, I will find the ancient book with the instructions for the sacred ritual.

I will take advantage of my new appearance and visit the Taíno village. I will become for them the feared monster that once again snatches an Indian girl in its claws to offer as a terrible sacrifice to my future Father.

I will transform into the avatar of the ancient legend of the snake-man who takes children, a story told by the light of a bonfire generation after generation.

I will turn into a monster, leaving those poor souls at the mercy of Yig. I will do everything I can to try to reverse my condition, to obtain the divine forgiveness of the Great Yig and, with his blessing, achieve redemption.

And in that endeavor, my sweet María will help me.

I will go in search of her. I will carry her over the hills and savannas like Zeus when he abducted the beautiful Europa.

And there, in the sacred cave where I killed Yig's Son, I will offer the Taíno girl and my precious María in sacrifice.

Once the Great Yig forgives me, satisfied by the innocent blood, I will seek out every hidden god I found mentioned in the apocryphal book.

I will push my sanity to the limits of the known world, praying to all those gods that no religion dares to mention. The All-in-One, The King in Yellow, The Black Goat of the Woods, The Crawling Chaos...

I will beg them all to grant me the knowledge to recover María's invaluable life, even if I must kill anyone in my way.

Even if I must sell my soul to the Court of Azathoth, the Idiot Chaos that gnaws and drools at the center of the infinite void.

I will do anything to bring her back to life, to remain forever by her side. I don't care what price I must pay.

But I am consumed by the fear that, upon waking from my long sleep, I will be nothing more than an elongated mass of gray scales, drooling fangs, and milky eyes. That is why I have written down my testimony and also drawn a map marking the location of the sacred cave, with its underground lagoon.

There, beneath the cold waters, on the rocky bottom, where the white bones of the dead buccaneers, the failed Baron, and the monumental serpent lie in a chaotic heap, more than ten quintals of gold and stolen jewels shine.

THE EARLY MORNING TRAIN

"Here comes the beast."

Yoric tensed his muscles and adjusted the straps of his backpack. Despite the ghostly lights dancing in the sky trying to confuse his senses, he had no doubt that the intense glow on the horizon was the Grasshopper.

The young man quickly glanced around to confirm he was the only person standing on the ten meters of concrete slab that served as a platform next to the solitary railway line.

"There's no chance it'll stop. Today, I'll have to board it."

Yoric mentally rehearsed the maneuver he had performed numerous times.

First, the powerful headlight of the locomotive appearing on the horizon would announce the approaching train. The light would disappear, swallowed by the dip in the terrain where the river produced a thick blanket of fog, only to reemerge with a shrill whistle, accelerating with all its might to overcome the slope.

That was a critical moment. If several people were waiting for the vehicle on the improvised platform, it increased the chances that a kind-hearted engineer would make a brief stop for the passengers to hurriedly board.

On the other hand, if only a few souls were watching the horizon, hoping to catch that form of public transport, the convoy would usually pass by, barely slowing down to respect the crossing a few meters from the end of the platform. After all, there was no official train station in that small village lost in the heart of the province. At least, not officially.

In the latter case, the only way to board the vehicle was to run as fast as possible, grab onto the handle of a door, and jump inside one of the cars before the train left the platform behind. There was no other option but to make a primitive boarding.

Due to these inconsistent stops, the early morning train had been nicknamed “Grasshopper”.

A successful boarding guaranteed a short trip of about forty minutes to the Central Station of the provincial capital, where, after a frantic race through the halls and platforms of the venerable building, it was possible to catch the university train and complete the journey to Central University, arriving with enough time to attend the first class of the morning. A luxury.

When the train's light disappeared into the fog tinged by the sky's mutating glows, Yoric crouched to warm up his joints and instinctively pulled his keychain from his pocket, kissing his good luck charm.

There was no one else around. People didn’t want to go out and expose themselves to the largest solar storm on record, which was causing auroras even in the tropical latitudes where the young man lived. That early morning, the sky looked like a witches' sabbath of ghostly lights.

Yoric didn’t care about the potential risks. Missing the train wasn’t an option because, in a few hours, he would have to face the final exam for Calculus II, for which he had studied so hard. Neither solar storms, nor auroras, nor even Hell itself opening up before him would stop him from getting there on time. He was going to board the Grasshopper at any cost.

The train emerged from the fog with a thunderous whistle, like an angry avatar of speed. That thing wasn’t going to stop.

Despite running with all his might, Yoric watched as the car doors escaped him one by one. The vehicle hadn't even slowed down slightly to respect the crossing. The end of the platform was approaching, and the opportunity to arrive in time for the final exam was slipping away by the second.

Without even thinking about what he was doing, Yoric leaped from the edge of the concrete slab. For a few seconds, he felt weightless, floating in the strangely illuminated early morning air. His hand reached the handlebar of the last door on the last car of the train, and his fingers wrapped around the cold steel.

The young man pulled with all the strength his arm muscles could generate, overcoming inertia and propelling his body into the dark interior of the vehicle. He slammed against the metal of the stairs and felt something break. His pain was eclipsed by a deep sense of euphoria and triumph. The boarding had been a success.

The young man was so ecstatic that he didn't even notice the light emerging from the fog rising from the river of his hometown. All of that was left behind at a dizzying speed.

With a violent jolt, the train let out another deafening whistle and accelerated again.

Yoric awkwardly got up and headed inside the car. As he limped through the dim light, he felt something sliding down inside his worn-out jeans. With sudden desperation, he checked the contents of his front pockets. Except for a hole through which his fingers slipped, there was nothing else there.

"Damn it!" he thought. "The impact against the stairs must have busted the bottom of my pockets."

When he bent down to try and retrieve his belongings, he felt something brush past his head, gently hitting his cheek.

With growing despair, he checked the state of his backpack. The pocket where he kept his wallet was open and empty.

"Great, things just keep getting better and better!"

Yoric resumed the task of feeling around the floor of the dimly lit car, trying not to think about the hygiene conditions of the place. The other passengers ignored him completely. Mentally, the young man took inventory of the lost items: five coins, three for the Grasshopper fare and two for the university train fare, the keychain with his good luck charm, and the wallet containing his ID and the money to last him the week.

With relative ease, he had already found some used chewing gum, two coins, and a few things he didn't even want to try identifying when he was surprised to see that his good luck charm was just a few steps away from his reach. The thing was glowing with a yellowish light he had never seen before. He crawled quickly to retrieve the object, but something made him stop dead in his tracks.

A sensation of deep horror ran through his entire nervous system. He felt the hairs on the back of his neck stand on end, as if he were under the influence of an electric field. With great effort, he controlled himself and looked up at the source of his strange feelings.

Crouched in front of him was what seemed to be a man. In the dim light, it was possible to make out that his lips weren't enough to cover some very large teeth protruding forward. A sparse and unkempt beard accompanied a mane of tangled and matted hair. The acidic and penetrating smell emanating from him raised serious doubts about his hygiene routine and the cleanliness of his clothes. In one of his hands, with uncomfortably long and neglected nails, he held Yoric's keychain. The charm swayed with the rhythm of the train's jolts; the design seemed to shine even brighter through the polished surface of the small teardrop-shaped stone.

—That's mine. —Yoric mumbled, extending his hand with the palm up.

—Of course, of course, —the stranger responded, and Yoric had the unpleasant sensation that instead of understanding the spoken words, their meaning formed directly in his mind. —What's yours is yours, —and he placed the keychain in the young man's palm.

Yoric clenched his fist around the object and withdrew his arm as quickly as he could. It seemed to him that the stone of his charm, always curiously cold, was now slightly warm. Avoiding looking at the figure in front of him, he put the keychain in the left chest pocket of his jacket and fastened the clasp to keep it secure.

—Welcome aboard the Worldhopper, José María Caraballo Robles, —the stranger continued.

—I prefer to be called Yoric, —the young man automatically replied, as he always did when someone called him by his first name. He then shuddered and looked up at his interlocutor. —How do you know my name?

The stranger now held Yoric's open wallet between his curved fingers. He smiled, and his teeth looked even more yellow and protruding toward the young man.

The young man snatched the wallet from the disconcerting figure with a quick movement. He immediately thought he was being rude. Although that guy was disturbing, he had found his lost items and, in a way, had returned them.

—Sorry for my rudeness, —Yoric said somewhat embarrassed as he stood up, —thank you for returning my things.

—There's nothing to apologize for. —The stranger replied, still crouched. —What's yours is yours, —and he began to laugh with a cackle that made the young man's skin crawl again.

Skirting the stranger, Yoric walked as quickly as he could toward the opposite end of the corridor. Only when the young man entered the next car did the roar of the train manage to drown out the unsettling laugh of the stranger in his ears. That made him feel a little better.

Most of the seats in that car were occupied. The passengers were shadowy figures, hard to distinguish in the ghostly light that trembled through the few open windows. Yoric's trained eyes spotted an empty seat at the far end of the car. He practically ran to occupy it and, driven by the conditioned reflex of someone who had spent many hours in crowded public transport and recognized the enormous advantage of sitting, he let himself fall into the hard seat.

He immediately began checking his belongings. With a mix of night vision, touch, and educated guesses, he concluded that nothing was missing from his wallet. His identification documents and the correct amount of bills were in their usual places. He checked that the pocket of his backpack where he usually kept his wallet wasn't torn; only the clasps had come undone from the impact, so he put the object away and securely closed the compartment.

He pulled his keychain out of his jacket pocket to check if the number of keys was correct. The small, polished teardrop-shaped stone that he considered his good luck charm hung from the short chain. The design embedded in it still seemed to glow with a faint yellowish light. As he focused his gaze on the unusual behavior of the object that had accompanied him since childhood, Yoric couldn't help but notice that the passenger sitting across from him was also looking at his charm.

That passenger was worth to looking at. He was dressed in white, with a suit, vest, tie, and gloves. Over his shoulders, he wore a long white trench coat that matched an elegant wide-brimmed felt hat adorned with an ivory-colored ribbon.

The entire outfit was absurdly elegant and luxurious, making Yoric wonder what a man so finely dressed was doing on the Grasshopper. He looked more closely at the man's face. The masculine features of the middle-aged black man were accentuated by well-groomed beard and mustache and reading glasses reflecting the flickering lights invading the car from the window.

In the gloved hands of the passenger was an open book, the cover of which Yoric couldn't distinguish. Out of pure politeness, the young man gave a slight nod of universal greeting while thinking,

"How is it possible for someone to read under these conditions?"

The passenger responded to the greeting with a similar gesture and returned to concentrating on his book.

Yoric resumed the task of inventorying his belongings, but something, creeping at the back of his mind, bothered him.

"This morning is quite unusual," Yoric thought without imagining that everything was about to get much worse.

—Tickets, please, —a voice resonated from the opposite end of the car.

In the corridor, a tall, thin figure, armed with a small flashlight, interacted with the shadowy passengers.

—If you haven't already bought your ticket, don't worry; you can purchase it now from me for the modest price of three coins.

Yoric put his keychain back in his jacket. Out of habit, he reached into his jeans for the ticket money only to find the torn bottoms of his pockets again.

"Oh, right," he thought, remembering the disastrous result of his unorthodox boarding. He pulled out the two remaining coins he had managed to recover from his jacket and stared at them, despondent, in the palm of his hand.

—The ticket costs three coins, —the elegant passenger across from him commented casually. The tone of the remark was a mix of indifference and condescendence.

Although the voice resonated deep and imposing, the young man again felt as if, more than hearing, the words of the character had formed directly in his mind. Ignoring the discomfort of being watched by his seatmate, the young man pulled a bill from his wallet.

—The conductor doesn't accept bills, only coins. —The passenger commented in the same tone.

—I take this train almost every week, —Yoric replied slightly annoyed, —and I've paid with bills several times.

—Excuse me, sir, but we don't accept bills, —came the voice of the conductor from the end of the corridor, —only coins, three coins, please.

Yoric raised his head abruptly. He strained his eyes to distinguish the conductor's figure, who was now engaged in a polite argument with a passenger refusing to accept his terms.

Something didn't feel right. That morning, the conductor was different. The employee was dressed in an anachronistic blue uniform with large, shiny metal buttons. The outfit included a cylindrical stiff cap with a patent leather visor and suede gloves.

Something didn't feel right. That morning, the conductor was different. The employee was dressed in an anachronistic blue uniform with large, shiny metal buttons. The outfit included a cylindrical stiff cap with a patent leather visor and suede gloves.

To increase the sense of discomfort, the figure's arms were disproportionately long, and the lenses of his round-framed glasses seemed to glow with a greenish light. The artificial smile on a mouth much longer than normal did nothing to restore the character's appearance of normalcy.

Suddenly, the passenger who was arguing with the conductor jumped into the corridor and ran toward the door behind Yoric. The young man clearly saw the expression of terror on the person's face as the conductor's gloved fingers grabbed them by the shoulders, stopping their run dead in its tracks. The passenger tried, without success, to grab onto something as they were dragged back to the other end of the car.

—Excuse me, sir, we don't accept bills, only coins. If you haven't already bought your ticket, you can purchase it now for just three coins, —the macabre employee's voice continued reciting.

—Three coins, —commented the deep voice of Yoric's elegant seatmate. —That's the price for traveling on the Worldhopper.

The young man put his two coins back in his jacket and picked up his backpack. He didn't like what he was about to do, but he had no other choice. He stood up from his seat, looking toward the opposite end of the car.

In the dim light, he could see the conductor's back walking stiffly, carrying the struggling and desperately screaming passenger by the shoulders, unable to break free. Yoric quickly walked in the opposite direction.

Yoric didn't like traveling without paying. It seemed deeply immoral to him, but he had done it before in extraordinary situations, and that early morning was beyond extraordinary. Where had those strange characters come from?

In the end, the trick to traveling without paying was relatively simple; you just had to avoid the conductor. You could walk ahead of the employee, and the train would eventually reach its destination before the conductor caught up with you. After all, the journey took about forty minutes, and the guy had to ask or collect the fare from each passenger.

"By the way, where am I?"

Yoric walked until he found an empty window seat. He sat down and peered through the cold glass. He tried to distinguish some reference point that would indicate where he was. Outside, there were only lights dancing chaotically and fog tinged with supernatural tones.

—By all the beating biting bitter demons...! —Yoric exclaimed aloud as he unconsciously pulled out his good luck charm.

—Are you afraid of demons?

The young man looked startled at the passenger who had made the comment. He was sitting in the seat across the aisle, with his arms crossed over his chest, displaying the largest biceps Yoric had ever seen in his life. The guy was wearing a sleeveless T-shirt that barely covered his muscular torso and sports pants. He was wearing dazzlingly white running shoes. His head was covered by one of those synthetic fabric beanies that rappers often wear. Even in the early morning gloom, he wore sporty sunglasses with elongated lenses illuminated by a perplexing reddish glow. The fleeing lights reflected off his dark, shiny skin. He moved his thick lips adorned by a mustache that connected to an equally fine and well-groomed goatee and casually commented:

—Demons rarely commute in the Worldhopper, and they always behave well while traveling here, so there's nothing to be afraid of.

The young man was about to say something, but at that moment, the light of a small flashlight shone at the entrance to the car.

"How did he get here so quickly?" Yoric wondered, almost panicking. He put away his charm and pulled out his two insufficient coins.

—Excuse me, —the young man said, half unsure, addressing his enormous neighbor, —can you break a bill into coins for me? I need coins to pay for the ticket...

The neighbor didn't even bother to look at him and snorted in disapproval.

—I don't have coins. Those who can't pay the price shouldn't even start the journey.

Yoric stood up again and continued his discreet escape. Before moving on to the next car, he looked back over his shoulder. Moving in his direction were the conductor's unsettling green lenses. The young man felt that the abnormally wide smile distorting the employee's face was directed at him.

The train continued at full speed, shaking the cars and their passengers. Yoric was completely baffled. By his calculations, several hours had already passed, and there had been no stop. Additionally, there were no signs of dawn.

The same spectacle of impossible and maddening lights continued through the windows.

What was happening this early morning? As he walked down the corridor of the cars, he replayed the strange encounters he had had on this insane journey.

“Why is everyone calling the Grasshopper as Worldhopper?”

—Tickets, please.

Yoric, almost overcome by panic, saw that the conductor was only a few meters away from him.

He pulled out his good luck charm and squeezed it tightly in his right hand as he started to run. He didn’t get far.

He ran straight into a muscular chest.

—You can’t pass this point.

Yoric blinked, confused in the dim light. In front of him, as massive as the bottom of the universe, was the passenger in sportswear and a rapper’s beanie, standing in front of a closed door with intense white light filtering through its windows. The muscular arms crossed over the titanic chest made it clear that this giant had no intention of moving.

The young man's mind tried to process how it was possible for that character to be standing there in front of him, but the conductor's voice repeating his litany crushed his ability to think.

—Please... Yoric mumbled, almost crying.

—Tickets, please.

The conductor was only a few steps away.

Yoric felt his strength leave him, and his knees began to buckle.

—Strength, let him in, please. Madness wants to ask him something, —came a voice from the other side of the closed door.

The giant huffed and stepped aside. The door opened, illuminating the corridor.

—Go ahead.

Yoric ran toward the light, and the giant followed him. The door closed behind them.

The young man's eyes took a few seconds to adjust to the intense brightness of the room. He blinked, confused, and looked around. This car was different, brightly lit, with no windows, and the walls were lined with metal shelves filled with small square safes. At the back, a massive circular armored door blocked the way. The space they were in was a small vestibule. On each side, next to each wall, there was a seat with its corresponding table.

In one of the seats was the first character Yoric had encountered that night, crouched. Under the bright light, his appearance was even more terrifying; he had ashen skin, tattered clothes, and completely white eyes, as if they were entirely taken by cataracts.

Yoric began to wonder how it was possible for that being to have read his documents in the dim light of the train, but the other occupant of the place caught his attention.

Sitting in the seat on the other side of the car was the exotic passenger elegantly dressed in white, still holding a book in his gloved hands.

Yoric was about to say something, but instead of articulating a word, the young man fell onto his own backside, overwhelmed by terror. He had just witnessed the exotic passenger pulling two more books from the inner pockets of his trench coat while the third volume floated in front of him.

Before the young man could recover, the terrifying figure jumped from his seat and crouched in front of him. Yoric searched desperately for an escape route with his eyes, but standing in front of the door he had entered was the titanic, muscular passenger with the rapper's beanie.

—José María Caraballo Robles, who prefers to be called Yoric, —began the crouched being, —can you show us your seed of curiosity and tell us how you obtained it?

—Excuse me, —Yoric mumbled, —I don't understand what you're talking about...

—The stone you use as a good look charm, —said the one dressed in white. —How did you obtain it?

Yoric pulled out the keychain. Without a doubt, despite the bright light in the room, the design embedded in the small teardrop-shaped stone was glowing with a yellowish light.

—This? It's a stone I found at the bottom of the river when I was like seven years old. It has this strange scribble that seems to have been etched inside it, but the surface is very smooth. When I found it, it even had a hole to thread a cord through it and use it as an ornament. Until this early morning, I had never seen this thing glow.

—You've never heard of the seeds of curiosity or the yellow sign? —asked the one dressed in white, consulting something in one of the floating books.

—I don't know what you're talking about. I didn't even know it was a known symbol; I always thought it was just an odd-shaped stain.

The figure standing by the door huffed, and Yoric felt the weight of his gaze on the back of his neck.

—Can we know why you boarded the Worldhopper today? —asked the terrifying one.

—I need to get to the university early. Today is the Calculus II final exam, and I've been studying like crazy for that exam for weeks. I can't be late.

The yellowed teeth of the blind one were even more exposed in what seemed like a smile. He began rocking from side to side like a chimpanzee while humming.

—Chase the learning, chase the learning, chase the learning, and it will be chasing you...—he suddenly stopped and looked at the one dressed in white with his milky eyes. —Knowledge, what do you think?"

—Those who diligently seek learning usually find the seeds of curiosity, though sometimes it's the other way around, —commented the one being addressed while consulting a line in one of his books. —Either way, they all end up in Carcosa... —a loud electric bell interrupted him. —Ah, yes, of course, that matter is pending. Strength, open the door, please.

The titan obeyed and stepped aside.

In the doorway, with his blue uniform with metal buttons, cylindrical stiff cap with a patent leather visor, flashlight hanging from his belt, suede gloves, and round-framed glasses with an intense green glow, appeared the conductor.

With a long stride, he planted himself right behind Yoric. He opened his abnormally long smile and extended a disturbingly disproportionate arm, with his palm facing up.

—Ticket, please. If you haven't already bought your ticket, don't worry; you can purchase it now from me for the modest price of three coins.

Yoric slowly got to his feet. He turned to face the smiling employee. He was trembling, and cold sweat beaded his forehead. With an unsteady hand, he placed his two coins in the conductor's extended palm.

The employee's smile widened even more, almost reaching his ears, and a row of white teeth gleamed sinisterly in the bright light.

—Three coins, —the voice sounded like the scraping of sharp steel pieces against each other.

Yoric sighed, ready to surrender to his fate when some curved fingers with long, neglected nails placed another coin in the conductor's palm. The young man blinked, confused.

—José María Caraballo Robles, are you sure you want to accept Madness' coin? —asked Knowledge in his deep voice.

—I prefer to be called Yoric, —the young man replied, — and yes, I accept.

The conductor ceremoniously stored the payment in a bag hanging from his belt. He pulled out a roll of tickets, tore one off, and handed it to Yoric.

—Enjoy your journey.

He turned and headed for the exit. Already in the doorway, he consulted a large pocket watch and announced,

—Next stop in two minutes.

He continued down the dimly lit corridor until he disappeared from view.

Yoric, still confused, looked down and read the recently purchased ticket. Stamped in green letters, it read: "WORLDHOPPER. One ticket."

—Can someone explain to me what's going on here? —he asked, not directing the question to anyone in particular.

At that moment, a shrill whistle was heard, and the train came to a sudden stop with a jolt.

—This is your stop, —said Madness, jumping back to his seat, where he crouched again. —I don't think you want to miss your stop.

Strength opened the door and gestured with his head, inviting the young man to leave. Yoric ran toward the exit.

—I hope we meet again, —Knowledge commented.

—I hope not, —the young man said as he crossed the threshold, and the door closed behind him.

—I'm certain we'll meet again, —Madness hummed as he rocked in his simian-like manner. —After all, you owe me a coin.

Yoric jumped onto the platform, which, as expected, was full of people hurrying along. He still felt disoriented, so he looked up, hoping to guess the time by the light of dawn.

To his disappointment, the sky was a mass of grays and lights dancing chaotically in preternatural tones.

The train he had disembarked from gave its usual shrill whistle and continued on its way, disappearing into thick fog.

Very irritated, Yoric searched for one of the information signs to try and locate himself. Bracing against the jostling of passersby, he spotted one of the white signs with black letters.

Elbowing his way through the crowd, he approached the sign to get a better view.

A chill ran down his spine, and cold sweat drenched his body. He was absolutely certain he would never make it to the exam he had studied so hard for.

Although he was sure he couldn't recognize the characters printed on the sign, his mind clearly understood what was written:

"Central Station of Carcosa".

LOST IN THE TAIGA

Once upon a time, there was a Cuban, a German, and two Spaniards. No, sorry to disappoint you, but this isn't one of those lousy jokes where three or four guys of different nationalities walk into a bar. The four men didn't stroll into a peaceful café after walking down an even more peaceful street, flirting with beautiful girls on the sidewalks.

The subjects of this story, myself included, entered a hellish boreal forest above the 58th parallel, in the middle of the harshest winter this century had seen, back in 1943. We had been sent to that white hell just to fight the Reds in their own Motherland, through the inscrutable wilderness of the Leningrad Oblast.

I've seen hundreds of men die in gruesome ways, both on the battlefield and in the gulag where I'm now imprisoned, but none of that compares to what we had the misfortune to deal with in those lost places, because it wasn't the Soviets who ravaged our bodies, minds, and souls, nor was it the intense cold. I wish it had been because what we faced, described in detail in this journal, was incomparably worse... it was the unknown.

February 13th...

—Look, —García pulled his hand out of his wool glove, showing me his hand, with the tips of his fingers starting to turn black from frostbite. —I can't feel them anymore. If it spreads, I'll have to cut them off.

Walter looked compassionately at the corporal's numb hands and willingly took off his gloves, offering them to García.

I never understood what someone with such a good heart was doing in a place like that. He must have been deceived by the same propaganda that fooled us. Walter could have been back in his native Bavaria, serving as a policeman, spending every night with his family, sleeping by the warm light of a fireplace.

Corporal García took them without saying a word, frowning. He despised pity from others, but he was well aware of his condition and knew that Walter didn't pity him. Instead, the German's blood was simply more accustomed to colder climates than the blood running through his Andalusian body, so a few hours of cold wouldn't bother him much. So, he swallowed his Iberian pride and, with his usual manner of a corporal with the airs of a sergeant, took the gloves without even offering thanks.

I watched the German's noble gesture and took the opportunity to rest for a moment from the weight I carried on my shoulders. The burden wasn't anything other than what I considered to be the biggest idiot in the Blue Division. Not only had he lost our invaluable MG42 somewhere only God knows, but he'd also been shot while peeing under a birch tree, giving away our position.

That's why I was carrying him on my back like a mule. At least it was my turn to do it at that moment.

Mateo, as the aforementioned *Gallego* was called, had an undeniable gift for scientific matters and such. But no one could rid him of the perpetual absent-mindedness he always carried with him, thus living up to the stereotype of cluelessness associated with the Galicia´s people, who is, in fact, far too courteous to be considered that way.

García and I met him at the train station that would take us to Germany for training. Together, we had laughed too much, lived, and seen a lot as well, to the point of considering each other brothers. We had practically walked from Poland to here, camping wherever possible and witnessing the atrocities of ghettos and concentration camps.

Novgorod was our baptism by fire. By the time winter had come, we managed to take the banks of the Volkhov to rescue a group of Germans holding out against enemy assaults. That's when we met Walter, a member of one of the weakest and most poorly prepared divisions of the Wehrmacht. He earned our affection by having saved his life, and he had been with us ever since. I had never met a more grateful person than him.

After that journey, we were directed to the outskirts of the city of Leningrad. The Russians had managed to break the nearly 900-day siege imposed by the Germans, and we received orders to take up defensive positions in Krasny Bor. It's understandable that, given the immense numerical superiority of the Soviets, our division was almost annihilated. Of the five thousand men remaining, half were wiped out.

A group of twenty men managed to escape into the frozen forest, and now only García, Walter, the injured *Gallego*, and I, Juanma, who is writing these lines and feeling like I'm going to die from hypothermia or in an ambush in this endless forest, are left. I leave my memories written on this diary, hoping that someday someone will find them in my cold hands and know that coming here was the worst decision. Dad, Mom... I always loved you all.

February 14th...

—Oh, how sweet! —García said as he took my small diary out of my coat pocket. —I didn't know you had a writer's side. Don't worry, I'd miss my parents too if they were alive.

I stood up, blushing, as I took back the little book he returned to me. Walter also laughed beneath the scarf covering half of his face. He had undoubtedly read my diary. Despite his mocking tone, García's expression was quite serious. He looked like a man visibly worried, but who somehow managed to boost the group's morale with his humor.

—Come on, Sleeping Beauty. There's more snow today than yesterday, and it'll be hard to walk with this fool on our backs, —he said, pointing at the wounded *Gallego*. —Let's build him a sled. Then we'll continue southwest.

After constructing the makeshift vehicle by tying long, sturdy branches with a rope and laying a tarp over it, we set off again. The snow that had fallen the previous night made our feet sink almost to our knees, slowing our progress considerably. About two hours later, we heard a loud explosion to the northwest, which put us on alert.

—Minefields, —Walter said, alarmed, but with his rifle slung over his shoulders and his arms resting on it like a scarecrow, giving the impression it wasn't that big of a deal.

—That's right. They're very close.

—The Russians? —I asked, cautiously running my hand along the strap of the rifle on my back.

—No, idiot. The mines.

—Coal mines? —Walter laughed.

—No, but they can certainly reduce you to less than a blackened chunk in the ground. So, Mr. Comedian, you stay here and look after *Gallego*. We'll go check it out. —García handed him his MP40 submachine gun. Walter's expression suddenly changed when he realized he'd be left alone with a wounded man in the middle of a forest surrounded by enemies. —Shoot anything that moves, and we'll hear you. Be careful with snipers, "miner".

From a distance, I saw poor Walter shudder, turning his head nervously under his stahlhelm, looking with pleading eyes, hoping we wouldn't abandon him there.

—Don't worry, —García said without even looking back, —we're just going to take a look. It could be our men retreating or the Russians stalking us. A little responsibility in solitude never hurt anyone.

—In a war, it does.

García fell silent and offered me a cigarette as we climbed a rise where the snow wasn't as thick, making it easier to walk. He knew I didn't smoke, yet he always annoyed me by offering me cigarettes when he didn't have an answer in a discussion.

—Look at that, —he said when we reached the forest clearing where the explosion had occurred, about two hundred meters from where we were.

—Dear God, —I was horrified by what we saw in the small crater formed by the blast.

—Well, neither ours nor theirs. Looks like the babushka went out to collect firewood and turned into charcoal, as Walter the comedian would say. Right, Juanma?

What we saw around the crater were the remains of a poor old woman who apparently had never evacuated her home. Of course, who would need to in a place so remote where one could easily get lost forever? Soviet partisans used such places to ambush us, but that wasn't the case here.

The body, still shrouded in the black smoke rising from the hole, lay face down. Her absent legs had probably been blown to splinters, along with her right forearm. Her torso, riddled with shrapnel from the mine and the surrounding rocks, was dressed in a brown *sarafan* under a black fur coat, and her head, like her legs, had been severed from her body and was nowhere to be found.

—Innocent people always pay the price...

—Let's go. Let's see how Walter fared in his mission.

Just as García finished his cold words, contrasting with my reaction to what we found, we heard a burst of machine-gun fire from where Walter and *Gallego* were.

—Damn it, speak of the devil...—García said just before we started running toward where we had left our companions.

We finally arrived, panting, our throats raw from the freezing air, at the spot where we had left Walter and *Gallego*.

Walter had been cautious, covering the sled with branches as camouflage. He had also taken up a position in the snow under some branches, with his helmet covered in a white tarp to avoid being seen by any enemy squad that might want to ambush them. When we saw him, he was standing with his coat dusted with frost and his weapon ready.

—Something attacked me, —he said.

—What was it?

—I don't know. It was some kind of animal. I've never seen a creature like it before; it was a small monster.

—Did it bite you? —I asked when I saw him holding his forearm, wincing in pain.

—Yes, it hurts like hell. I don't know what that thing was, but I managed to shoot it. It ran off in that direction.

Walter pointed to a trail of strange black liquid with reddish iridescence left in the fresh snow. The tracks looked like bird footprints, perhaps a chicken. But there were two sets of marks, suggesting there were two animals.

—Don't tell me you were attacked by a pair of wild chickens, Walter, you idiot, —García said disdainfully, pressing his thumb and forefinger to his brow as if suffering from a severe headache.

—Do you think a chicken could have done this to me? —he pulled up the sleeve of his coat, visibly offended at having his story doubted. He showed us a wound that looked like it had been made by a small dog, with the morbid detail of a bifurcation in the middle, suggesting a deformity in the animal's jaw.

—The enemy might have heard the gunfire from several kilometers away. You should have used the knife, —I reprimanded, trying to ignore the strangeness of the wound.

—Follow that black trail, —he said, barely acknowledging my criticism. —I'm not looking at that thing again.

Curiosity piqued; we followed the strange creature's trail left by our companion.

—If it's a chicken or an ermine, I'll treat your wound with a cigarette! —shouted García as he set off, to which Walter sarcastically replied...

—I was just following orders, sir: 'Shoot anything that moves!' Remember? I think a varmint attack counts as movement, Corporal!

—Oh, shut up, you bloody German! —the hysterical urge to laugh from their argument evaporated when I saw the thing lying shot to pieces on the snow.

—Do you know anything about biology, García? —I asked, half-joking and half-afraid, in a pathetic attempt to imitate my friend's jolly nature in the face of adversity.

—No idea, —he replied, flipping off Walter as he turned around. —Why do you ask...? Holy Mother of God, what hellhole did this beast crawl out of?

Even García, the man with nerves of steel, jumped back in disgust as he looked at what appeared to be a hairless ferret but with four chicken legs covered in bluish-gray skin. Its head was twisted to the side, and it had two upper jaws, explaining Walter's wound. Additionally, for some inexplicable reason, it had horrific blackish tentacles on its sides. It lay in a shimmering black puddle of its own blood.

Only God knows what kind of rabies that monstrosity could have infected Walter with, so when we returned, we disinfected his wound with alcohol and bandaged him. After telling him what had happened, we decided to head back toward the minefield. Perhaps the old woman's house wasn't far from there, and we'd have shelter for the night.

To our infinite surprise, we found the crater empty. The mutilated body was gone. Instead, there was a large splash of what had appeared to be blood a few minutes ago but now was a dark, iridescent stain.

—It's the same blood as that thing, —Walter's voice trembled, and not from the cold.

—Shut up. How could it be the same? —García replied, having no idea how the lifeless body had disappeared. —How many people do you know who can run away without a head and legs after an explosion like that?

—I wasn't suggesting it ran away, —I interjected, equally baffled. —There wouldn't have been time for the blood to coagulate like this. Besides, coagulated blood doesn't have this hue. It's identical to that strange creature's blood.

—Something's not right in this place. —Walter looked around as if expecting something unspeakable to emerge from the silent trees. García, in his eternally skeptical and sarcastic tone, retorted...

—You're right. And do you know what's not going well? Look down and answer yourself. We're in a damn minefield! This isn't the time for witch tales! Maybe a scavenger took the old woman. And the blood... maybe she drank ammonia or something, who knows. What matters now is figuring out how to get out of here.

—If we follow the old woman's tracks, we'll get out safely. —My comment seemed to calm García for the moment, until I voiced my observation out loud: —But notice one thing. The tracks go up to the mine, but there are none showing that she fled or was dragged away by an animal or person. Nothing, it's as if...

—As if she flew away? —the voice came from the sled, where *Gallego* lay under a thick blanket. He was conscious and apparently had overheard our conversation.

The atmosphere thickened, and light snowflakes began to fall. After trudging for about five hours, the curtains of towering pines and birches seemed endless.

—Well, look who's awake. Let's leave Baba Yaga to fly around the pines and focus on getting out of this trap alive.

We crossed the dangerous clearing along the same footsteps the old woman had left and entered the forest again, into an even denser and darker section than before, so much so that the light filtered through the frozen branches in thin beams. The air also felt heavier than usual, and I sensed an odd aura, unlike anything my senses had ever perceived before, as if my comrades were bathed in some strange emanation from the forest itself.

The atmosphere thickened, and light snowflakes began to fall. After trudging for about five hours, the curtains of towering pines and birches seemed endless.

The universe seemed to shrink into an eternal and ominous forest, a growing snowstorm, and four half-dead men. Two of them were in poor shape, as Walter was beginning to suffer from a fever accompanied by strange hallucinations, according to him. It was likely due to the bite from that amorphous little creature.

We wanted to find the old woman's house, but we had lost her trail long ago. The continuously falling snow had erased all the footprints.

After what felt like endless hours of wandering through the forest, we came upon a clearing where, some time ago, a Luftwaffe Heinkel 111 had crashed. Thinking it might contain provisions or ammunition, we decided to spend the night there without lighting any fire. It would be a colossal blunder to start a fire in our current situation for obvious reasons, though the increasingly hostile weather seemed to promise a brutal snowstorm overnight.

We approached the crash site. The tops of the nearby trees were sheared off from north to south. The plane had likely come from somewhere near the capital of the oblast or from the Karelian Isthmus, chased by Russian fighters that brought it down here.

In the cockpit, the two pilots were dead in their seats. They had died instantly upon impact, and their bodies were frozen. We pulled them out of the aircraft and proceeded to rummage through the wreckage for anything useful, food or medicine for *Gallego* and for the increasingly weak and delirious Walter.

The Heinkel was leaning to one side, with one wing in the air and the other completely shattered on the ground. The cockpit windows were all broken, and the fuselage was riddled with bullet and shrapnel marks. Inside, we found two moldy loaves of bread, a small first-aid kit, and several boxes of ammunition for the MG13 machine guns mounted on the plane. The bomb compartment was also completely empty.

It wasn't one of those warm Slavic *isbas* with the cozy glow of a fireplace, but it was better than being out in the elements. So, we camped there.

That night, the weather didn't improve. It had been snowing all afternoon, and by dawn, the blizzard had reached its peak. The metal frame of the plane blocked the wind, but it didn't insulate us from the cold.

Once settled into our improvised shelter, we had changed the *Gallego*'s bandages and disinfected Walter's wound.

The rock-hard, expired loaves of bread looked pitiful, but we were so hungry that we devoured them as if they were a feast. While we ate, García kept watch through the shattered windows.

—It doesn't look like it'll let up until tomorrow. I closed the cockpit door because the wind coming through the broken window felt like the devil himself was blowing outside. Here, cripple, —the corporal said, rubbing his hands and taking off his gloves to give them back to Walter. —The pilots of this scrap heap won't need gloves anymore, so I borrowed them. Thanks.

But Walter didn't hear him, lost in a disturbing stupor that made him mutter like a dying man. His hands, which had been rosy and healthy this morning, had turned pale and veiny, marked with bluish veins.

Gallego slept while Walter repeated the same litanies, half in German and half in Spanish, shivering from fever and cold.

—I'm so scared. She's marked me. Her deformed offspring did it. The six hundred adore her... *Die schwarze Ziege des Waldes*. I'm not dying, I'm transforming. Gott... *hilf mir*.

The nonsense he was saying chilled my blood more than the fifty below zero temperatures seeping in through the turret's skylight. His physical and mental health had deteriorated quickly since that little beast attacked him. I could hardly recognize him anymore due to his condition.

—Hey, Juanma, come take a look at this.

García suddenly stood up from the window and peered out through the turret's windshield, alerted by something he had seen outside. I stood up, eager to know what had caught his attention, but as I did, Walter grabbed my arm in desperation, pleading for me to stay by his side. Walter wasn't just trembling from the cold or his fever. He was trembling with terror, and I could feel it through his hand.

—*Nain!*... Don't let it take me! It's coming for me! I've been marked by her! My God, Juanma, don't leave me! Don't let them take me to the Void with the drums and the flutes! *Nain, bitte!*

—What's wrong with you? Try to calm down, or you'll give us away! —I managed to pull free from his grasp, and he was left rocking back and forth in his blankets, banging his head against the metal wall.

Now standing next to García, he pointed to a spot in the distance. I squinted in that direction and saw two small white dots, like the eyes of a nocturnal animal.

—Do you think it's a deer? —I asked.

—At this hour, in this weather...?

—It can't be a bear either. They hibernate this time of year.

As if in response to my speculation, Walter began screaming frantically, thrashing like a wild animal caught by a predator.

—It's her, it's her! Shoot her, do whatever it takes, but don't let her catch me! She knows I'm here, and she's coming for me!

—Shut up already, damn it! —García ordered on the verge of losing his temper. Walter half-obeyed the corporal's commanding voice, returning to his feverish muttering.

We continued to stare in the direction of the two glowing dots shining through the snowstorm, and this time we could make out a strange silhouette behind them. A shadow of what looked like a small tree that hadn't been there before and, more importantly, appeared to be moving. Furthermore, the shape of the supposed tree didn't match the conifers of the region. It didn't resemble anything we'd ever seen before.

After a few seconds, the two glowing eyes shifted, and we were stunned to see a silhouette. It wasn't a bear or a deer, but a person. It was impossible for anyone to be alone in the middle of nowhere in such a bitter cold.

Yet there it was, nearly indistinguishable, scanning the wreckage of the plane where we sought shelter from the freezing night. I felt, down to my bones, that in some morbid way, it knew we were there and took satisfaction in the fact that we had no idea of its intentions.

—If it gets any closer, I'll shoot.

García raised his weapon, and I did the same. We both aimed at whatever was out there, unnerved by Walter's delirious voice in the background. Even *Gallego* woke up at that moment.

As if sensing our intentions, the figure watching us from outside slunk away into the darkness like a corrupted spirit of the woods. We lowered our weapons, Walter calmed down a little, *Gallego* went back to sleep like a dormouse, and I sat by the cabin door, finally exhaling.

García, who was less detail-oriented than I, didn't seem to notice the shadow of the tree standing beyond those eyes. It was overwhelming to look out there, where there was nothing for miles, and you couldn't see beyond your nose, so I resolved not to do it again. Everything seemed like an eternal yet depressing calm for a few minutes.

Walter, along with *Gallego*, had also fallen asleep under a thick aviator's coat we had taken from one of the dead pilots. García poured water from his canteen onto a cloth and placed it on his forehead. Then he sat beside me with a cigarette in hand.

—I'm not keeping watch anymore. With this weather, not even the Russians would dare search for anyone out here. All we want is to sleep, right?

—Yes. It hasn't been easy dragging this idiot *Gallego* around all day. But what if the snowstorm ends, and we're still asleep?

—Well, we'll see.

With that carefree statement, García took his blanket, curled up on one side, and soon fell asleep.

Now I'm the only one awake, listening to the wind howling over the metal frame of the plane. The icy whistle and the snores of my three companions are the only sounds accompanying me, lulling me into thoughts of the vastness surrounding us, like being in a submarine submerged in the dark waters of the ocean.

What we saw outside gave me a sense of terrifying familiarity, as if we had seen it before. The malignant malevolence of that presence seemed too vast to belong to this world, yet there it was, stalking us like a predator watching its prey.

I just hope with all my heart that thing doesn't appear again tonight. The missing old woman's corpse, the abominable creature that bit Walter, the iridescent blood, and the two strange figures outside our refuge. Walter was right back in that minefield. Something is very wrong in these woods.

February 15th. 4:30 P.M...

This morning, the sky was studded with gray and opalescent clouds. The storm likely stopped just before dawn, and the snow had piled up heavily on the wings of the plane and the branches of the pines. Everything was quiet to the point of exasperation. The robins and blackbirds chirped faintly in the nearby groves, and the light breeze rustled the torn metal scraps on the tail fin of the Heinkel, gently shaking the ice-laden birch treetops in the same manner.

Walter had died during the night.

The event hit me hard. Everything around me remained in a sort of limbo.

Walter had been an excellent comrade and bore a kindness that didn't fit the world's stereotype of a Nazi. Even García knew this and felt the sad absence of such a jovial person.

—How did he die?

—Hypothermia and rabies, or a mix of both, I don't know. He was having a lot of hallucinations before he died.

—It all started after that creature bit him. But rabies doesn't kill that fast. I'll examine the body.

—I already buried him.

—Where did you bury him?

—What does it matter? He's dead.

—But I can still examine him.

—Are you a doctor? Why do you want to examine him? —García spoke with his back to me, smoking another cigarette. His evasive way of communicating awakened something in my mind, telling me he was hiding something about Walter's death.

—García... is there something you're not telling me?

He lowered his head and dropped the cigarette, which sank into the snow, melting it with its heat.

—García...—I insisted, approaching him and grabbing him by the sleeve of his coat. —What happened to Walter? What did you do to him? Answer me! Speak, García... what are you hiding?!

—Nothing, man, nothing! Are you implying I killed him?! That I got rid of him because an injured man, a sick man, would be a burden?! Do you think I'd kill a sick person like some damn Nazi, thinking he was weak?!

—Then answer me! How did he die? —By the time I asked him this, tempers had flared, and we were shouting at each other, grabbing each other by the collar, arguing like madmen in the spectral silence of the forest. Only then did I lower my voice, fearing that a partisan patrol might hear us because of my outburst. —Is it so hard to explain?

—I woke up pretty late when the snowstorm ended. He was lying in the same corner where you last saw him. None of the medicine in the kit was helping him anymore. In fact, they seemed to make his condition worse. When I checked his wound, it was very dark, and he wouldn't stop babbling, saying he was seeing and hearing things... something about a black goat. Later, he convulsed and tried to scream, but collapsed into the blankets and never got up again... ever. After that, I took him outside and buried him next to the other two Germans. That's it, I swear to you, Juanma.

His voice wasn't the usual hardened tone I was used to. Instead, it was the saddest I'd ever heard, and his eyes were more sorrowful than I'd ever seen in him. For a moment, I believed him. But a doubt arose. Why did Walter try to scream but couldn't, according to García? What had stopped him from doing so? Did he choke on his own spasms? Or could it be that García...?

—Do you hear that? We need to get inside the plane, now!

García cut off my thoughts, forcing me to listen briefly to what had alerted his senses. I could hear the faint but growing rumble of engines approaching. It wasn't coming from within the forest. The sound came from the air.

—Move it, you idiot, they're going to see you!

I was frozen for a moment until García's shout snapped me out of it. I sprinted back to our rusty refuge. We stared at the sky, filled with the buzzing of Sturmovik reconnaissance and assault planes flying through the opalescent sky, probably searching for retreating enemies like us. We cautiously watched them pass over the glass dome of the turret.

From the ground, they looked like massive steel crosses flying overhead. If they spotted us, they could turn us to pulp with their powerful machine guns.

—We need to leave now, —García said once the entire air squadron had passed. —The Russians were waiting for the storm to end to continue advancing. Soon the tanks will be near.

Before we could even hear the terrifying roar of the tanks, we had already set off through the taiga once again. We dragged the injured *Gallego* on the sled as quickly as we could.

As we ventured deeper into the forest, heading west, I felt the strange, dark aura covering this desolate place like a shroud growing more vivid with each step. It was as if I constantly felt an insidious gaze hidden among the cold trunks. Like the ominous eyes that had stalked us through the snowstorm the night before.

With Walter's death, this sensation intensified. It felt as if the soul of the deceased was haunting us, trying to warn us of something truly horrible lying ahead, wherever we were heading now. Something he might have been trying to warn us about just before he lost his life.

February 16th. Late at night...

Yesterday morning, we left the ruins of the Heinkel with the Red Army almost on our heels. The endless groves we passed through all day seemed to close in more and more, as if even the pines and larches of the area were immobile comrades of the Russians, carrying out their mission to make our progress more difficult.

Near dusk, we stopped hearing the distant rumble of tanks. Apparently, not only were they struggling to advance alongside the infantry in such rugged terrain, but like us, they saw that it was starting to snow again.

Although García seemed to assume the enemy would camp at a safe distance, he ordered us to keep moving until well into the night to put even more distance between us and them. Then it would be the right time to set up camp under a rock or between the roots of a tree.

Suddenly, a house appeared before us.

We had long since given up hope of finding the cottage of the woman from the minefield, having lost her trail. We were too far from the place where we thought the babushka had met her explosive end. We were so far from the minefield that, at first, we thought this *isba* must belong to someone else.

The structure stood in a clearing in the middle of nowhere. Supported by what had once been four trees, whose trunks had been cut at a rather uncomfortable height to chop them down with an ax, the solitary cabin stood, built with birch wood. The rooted trunks that served as its foundation gave the impression of colossal chickens hidden in the hut, their legs left exposed.

A shiver ran down my spine as the grotesque creature whose bite had led to Walter's death came to mind.

Icicles hung in front of the closed door. The porches and windows were shut too. No smoke came from the chimney. Confident that no one occupied the place, we decided to enter.

But something caught our attention powerfully. As we climbed the steps leading to the elevated porch, we heard a disdainful bleat coming from the back of the cabin. While García continued toward the door of the cabin, I went to investigate.

—Hey, García, come look at this.

—What?

It was a goat tied to one of the "legs" of the house. The animal had pitch-black fur, contrasting with the surroundings like a blot of tar on a pristine white shirt. It's a bit absurd to say, but the creature had piercing eyes. Behind its rectangular pupils, it gave the impression of possessing an almost human degree of intelligence.

The animal's eyes seemed to invite us into the cabin. All with that same aura of malignancy I had noticed along the entire way. García, of course, with a coarser mindset than mine, perceived nothing and, watching the animal, snapped me out of my strange meditation by saying...

—Well, well. What are you staring at this thing for? Don't tell me you've fallen in love with the goat?

—What are you talking about, man...? It just seems strange that if no one lives here, this goat wouldn't be out in the open. Or it wouldn't be alive by now.

—Maybe they couldn't take it with them when they fled.

—Fled? From their own people? It's more likely that whoever lives here just went out into the woods.

—For what? A stroll with the dog?

García was already starting to pull out a cigarette to smoke it, ready to offer me one of them when he ran out of answers. His attitude was really starting to annoy me at that moment, a feeling that had been growing worse since we left the plane... since poor Walter died.

—Going out to gather firewood and put it in the stove to avoid freezing to death at night doesn't seem like a good enough reason to you?

—All that seems to me is that we've got food and shelter for the night! When the imaginary owner of the house returns, we'll force him to give us shelter and not betray us to the Reds.

—So now it suits you to be a damn Nazi?! To extort and force the 'inferior' ones to your convenience?! 'The plague isn't red, it's brown, and we're part of it'! Now I truly understand why you mention it occasionally.

—That's enough!

Without realizing it, our conversation had escalated to the point where we were shouting at each other, with the black animal standing in front of us, watching us passively.

I wanted to throw everything I was thinking in García's face. I wanted to tell him that he wasn't the same person I had met back in Spain. I wanted to reproach him for how the constant presence of death and barbarism had frozen his soul and dulled his mind. But what burned my blood the most was the desire to express my suspicions about him regarding Walter's final moments.

So many things that disappointed and angered me wrestled within me, tying a knot in my throat, wanting to finally burst into words that would release my damn frustration. I was about to do it, but the fearful and pleading voice of *Gallego* reached us from the front porch, where he lay on the wooden floorboards. We ran to his aid, leaving our unfinished argument behind.

The poor man was muttering, terrified, nearly unintelligible words under the effects of the fever from his wound. His last phrase caused me a terrible unease that manifested in a violent shiver, as if my coat had been suddenly ripped off in the freezing winter twilight...

—No. Stay away from me... I don't want to go, please... She's here... *Iä Sh... Shub... Shub N...* Those aren't trees, they're her cursed offspring... stay away from her... The Black Goat of the Woods.

A shiver ran down my spine, and goosebumps covered my skin. Walter had also mentioned a black goat in the woods during his delirium, just hours before he died, right when we saw the disturbing glowing eyes outside the ruins of the plane. Now we were faced with an animal with the exact characteristics in the backyard of the *isba*.

How had *Gallego* managed to guess so accurately that there was a black goat nearby? It would be nearly impossible for him to have seen it because the animal was on the opposite side of the property. He was lying on the wooden porch, barely able to get up on his own. The whole situation was deeply unsettling. The fact that the words of his delirium eerily coincided with those of the late Walter, just as that malevolent presence had appeared, made everything far more terrifying.

It chilled me to think that the events of that moment, the previous night, and even those of the morning before were abominably connected.

Something very sinister was circling everything we had experienced in recent days. Things that somehow intertwined, giving me the vague impression that this *isba* was the epicenter of all these events.

Neither the house nor the forest generated any positive feelings in me, much less now. But between wandering through the forest at night in sub-zero temperatures and having a roof over our heads, surrounded by four walls, the choice was more than obvious. We entered the cabin and laid *Gallego* down on a rough bed made of furs.

In the living room, there were some birch furniture on a bison hide rug. The kitchen was part of the living room, with a wood stove surrounded by copper cauldrons hanging from the walls next to a worn-out cuckoo clock. We were struck by the fact that both the stove and the oven were off. Nearby, there was a large stack of firewood.

The mystery surrounding the owner's absence only grew for me. Night had already fallen over the taiga, and the owner of the *isba* had not returned. It was clear that they didn't need to go out looking for firewood. They already had plenty.

So, what on earth had the mysterious owner gone into a forest that extended for endless miles without any sign of a town or village? When I voiced my concerns to García, he gave me a fairly logical answer.

He said that perhaps the person who lived here had seen us at some point in the afternoon and had run off to where the Russian troops were camped to report us to them. If that were true, then we needed to be especially cautious. But by this point, I already suspected that there were far worse things in these parts than falling into the hands of the Russians.

I wanted to convince myself that the owner was nothing more than a simple hermit loyal to Stalin who had run off to betray our position to the Reds. However, everything around me screamed that whoever lived here was anything but ordinary or simple.

Painted and scratched on the walls, we saw all sorts of runic hieroglyphs and strange things tied with strings. Bones, twigs, feathers, and skulls of small birds and rodents were arranged to form bewildering symbols. In every corner, there were small golden candelabras adorned with inscriptions in an unknown dialect, drawn with a strange iridescent black substance. A cabinet filled with jars of eggs, herbs, spices, and rare stones from the forest, interspersed with books of incalculable antiquity, particularly caught my attention.

This didn't seem like the home of a modest Russian peasant but of a hermit sorcerer completely cut off from the world. Nothing there gave me a good feeling, least of all that goat in the yard, which García, in his total lack of common sense, insisted on bringing inside the cabin.

The proximity of the creature didn't inspire any good feelings in me. On the contrary, the animal seemed to exert a malevolent influence on *Gallego*, who, with his eyes closed, struggled in his feverish delirium, constantly mentioning the black goat he hadn't even seen.

The situation chilled me to the bone. The entire negative energy of the forest seemed to bubble up from this place. From that animal. It's easy to imagine the look on my face when García said we'd eat it right there, that very night.

He crossed the house and, without warning, headed to the yard. He told me he was going to bring the creature, but he didn't mention whether he'd bring it alive or dead. A while later, *Gallego* suddenly entered a frenzied state, causing the damp cloth on his forehead to fall to the ground. The injured man rose, as if waking up in his own coffin, shouting things that made my hair stand on end.

—What have you done?! You shouldn't have killed it, now we're doomed! Don't you understand?!... That cursed animal... *Iä Iä Shub Niggurath!* The Black Goat of the Woods... she'll curse us!

—Gallego, you need to calm down. Who are you talking about? No one has killed anyone.

—He did. He killed her vessel. Let's flee now while we still can. Shub Niggurath, she's coming for us, Juanma. She wants to take us to the Court of the Sultan of Demons to dance eternally to the rhythm of the drums and flutes... in the Infinite Void!

I was completely stunned and horrified by the *Gallego*'s incoherent babbling, unable to offer him any comforting words. He was out of his mind, speaking of horrible things about unknown gods and someone named Shub Niggurath, and... in a terrifying twist, he predicted what was happening outside, far beyond our view...

—What's going on here? —García entered, perplexed, with the slaughtered goat on his shoulders. How *Gallego* had once again hit the mark in the midst of his delirium, I didn't know. But there was García, the idiot, with the animal's body, ready to prepare it for our meal.

—What do you think you've done, you piece of crap?

—Watch how you talk to me, you little piece of filth, —he shot me a menacing look, speaking in a low voice, gritting his teeth.

—Why did you kill the goat?! We have no right to sacrifice someone else's livestock, you damned Nazi!

—I did it for the three of us, you colossal fool! What do you prefer? Starving to death or letting some brute of a peasant enjoy his bastard goat for another day? We had no choice!

Not an hour had passed before we were arguing again. The most intense argument we'd had so far. The concert of shouts and insults, in tune with the delirious ranting of *Gallego*, made the atmosphere more hostile by the minute. The injured man half-sat up this time, accusing García with infinite anger and terror for his misdeed.

—You! You, you brainless idiot! Stay away from us with your curse! You're going to die, you bastard! You shouldn't have killed her!

—What's wrong with you, you useless bedwetter?!

—Shub Niggurath will claim you. She's closer than you think. You won't drag us down with you.

—Juanma, this guy has really lost it.

—I don't think so, —was all I could say in a strange tone before *Gallego* reached for his belt, looking for his pistol.

—You're the only one responsible for what you just did. Your soul is lost, but I won't let Shub Niggurath take us down with you. I'll make sure you don't suffer a worse end than the one I'll give you, García.

—Who the hell is Shub... are you threatening me, you lunatic?

Gallego pulled his P38 from his belt and aimed it at García, who reacted quickly before the injured man could lift the gun. The corporal delivered a swift blow to his forehead with the butt of his rifle, knocking the wounded man unconscious again.

—What did you do to him?! —I protested, rushing to *Gallego* to check the severity of the blow.

—What did I do to him? The question is, what would this maniac have done to me? —he replied, picking up the weapon from the injured man's hands.

He moved away from the sofa, not even looking at me, and said as he headed toward the body of the animal lying on the ground, —Don't just stand there. Help me prepare this.

I was unpleasantly surprised that, despite everything that had happened, he was still thinking about eating that damned animal.

—Why the hell didn't you tell me before?

—What are you talking about?

—You know perfectly well. Even the ineptest person would know something's very wrong here, in this place and these woods. —I spoke firmly, with clenched fists, waiting for any reaction from García, who turned defiantly, sensing that I was verbally offending him.

—Are you calling me inept?

—Since yesterday, things have been happening that we've tried to ignore, —I continued. —You keep clinging to the idea that nothing's wrong. The body that disappeared in the minefield, the creature that bit Walter and supposedly caused his death...

—What do you mean by 'supposedly'? —he interrupted, realizing I was accusing him. —Don't tell me you believe in witch tales too, Juanma. I expected that from this unfortunate *Gallego* and from Walter as well. But from you? Damn, how low you've fallen.

—You're the one who's fallen low. And do you know why? Yes, you know it well... You killed Walter, didn't you?

—Stop talking nonsense and help me with the goat.

—You're still going on about the goat?!— my jaw clenched so tight that my teeth hurt.

The words escaped from between my teeth, which I was grinding until it was painful. The man standing before me was no longer a man. He was a cold, arrogant thing I once admired. A despotic murderer who didn't even take me seriously. That cold thing unleashed the burning knot that had been choking me, turning it into a shout of rage.

—You killed him, damn it! —I don't know how, but I already had the pistol in my hand. All I remember from that moment is that everything I saw was tinted in a deep red. —You decided he was too weak to drag along with *Gallego* because one sick man was enough! That's why he couldn't scream... you stifled his cries so he would die in his sleep, without even seeing your face, you damned coward! —García raised his arms, and this time he did take me seriously. In fact, I dare say it was one of the very rare times I saw fear in his eyes.

—Juanma... lower the gun. I'll explain everything if you do. Please, don't do something foolish.

—I don't want to hear your explanations. You've lied enough. Stop ignoring reality. You killed the goat, and we didn't even hear it cry for its life. Do you think that's normal? And before you came in with the dead animal, *Gallego* already knew. He knows something about all of this that we're missing. Walter knew it too.

—They were both delirious! Do you have any idea how high their fevers were? —he lowered his voice after asking the question. —I did it for our own good, Juanma... so we wouldn't starve to death, damn it. What they said was pure coincidence.

—Two people deliriously repeating the same thing several times is too much of a coincidence, —I retorted as I cocked the gun. —You're going to get rid of the animal right now. It looks really strange. Something's wrong with it, and I can't let you cook it.

García obeyed my order, bending down silently to pick up the goat's body, with his back turned to me. Then, grabbing it by one of the legs, he spun around like lightning and hit me with the dead beast. Instinctively, I fired, and the bullet hit a pot, making it clang.

The blow was strong, leaving me half-bent for a moment. García took advantage of the situation to kick me in the ribs, knocking the pistol far from my reach. As García approached to continue beating me, I managed to sweep my leg under his ankles, causing him to fall heavily on his side.

He tried to grab the wooden table for support but only managed to knock over the rifle that had been resting on it. I seized the moment, while he was down, to mount him and unleash all my anger on his face with my fists.

The red haze in my vision grew deeper. I had never felt so furious and disappointed as I did at that moment. But deep down, I felt happy. I felt as if I were releasing the brave and dignified soul of García from the empty, cruel shell he had become. I also felt as if I were avenging Walter, who had been so kind to us, especially to García, lending him his own gloves so his fingers wouldn't freeze.

Lost in my frenzy, seeing that I couldn't knock out García, I failed to notice his hand stretching laboriously to grab the rifle from the floor and hit me over the head with it. I fell backward, and in an instant, the roles reversed.

Now García was my attacker. His face was as hard as a boxer's, spitting and bleeding from his nose. My face, on the other hand, couldn't withstand as much. After three punches, I was seeing stars, and another three were enough to make me forget everything until I woke up, semi-dazed, with a faint smell of roasted meat.

I felt a pleasant warmth, accompanied by an amber light bathing my half-closed eyes. I was still on the floor, at the foot of the table, where I saw García's boots and pants. I could hear him crunching something, chewing. On the bed, I saw *Gallego* lying down, and I noticed that he was tied to it, sobbing quietly with the damp cloth on his forehead. García had lit the stove and oven to warm the room and cook whatever smelled so good. I noticed García standing up and leaning toward me.

—Good evening, Sleeping Beauty. Would you like to eat?

I got up without him trying to stop me. He hadn't even tied me up. He knew me so well that he knew I wouldn't challenge him again, as he was far more skilled and stronger than me. He kept talking nonchalantly, even after all of this. That disgusted me deeply. That arrogant person who was no longer the friend I once knew.

I didn't answer him at all. Neither did he. His attitude was like that of a father patiently waiting for his child to get over their tantrum, and I hated him for it. I hated him seriously.

I stumbled over to the table and looked at García's pot, empty except for the remnants of bones and cartilage at the bottom. I turned to García with a look of contempt and reproach on my numb face.

—Tell me you didn't do it.

—What are you talking about? —he replied cynically, licking his fingers.

My anger toward him grew, and I decided not to speak another word to him. In response to his irritating question, I merely took the empty pot and let it drop accusingly onto the wooden floor. García, pretending not to notice, rolled a cigarette. He knew me like no one else, but I knew him too. I knew he was about to offer me a cigarette.

—Light the damn cigarette and swallow it if you want, —was all I managed to say, gritting my teeth. Before my vision turned red again, I headed for the door. García just shrugged silently and said as I left...

—There's no need to keep watch outside, man, but if you're going out for some fresh air, close the door, damn it, you're letting the heat out.

That, along with the *Gallego*'s low, sobbing voice repeatedly saying, —She's here, she's here, —like a gloomy warning, was the last thing I heard before I lifted my head and froze in terror when I saw those two figures in the night under the snowfall, just a few meters in front of the cabin. Two spectral images in the darkness that, if I make it out of this alive, I'll never erase from my mind.

Before me materialized the glowing eyes we had seen back at the plane wreckage, but this time they were much closer. But even more terrifying was the person with those eyes.

The brown *sarafan*, the black fur coat, and the shape of the body, which I saw thanks to the yellowish light coming from the open door. That woman, that old lady who lay in the minefield, without legs, without a head... was now standing right in front of me, with all her limbs intact!

I knew it was her, looking at me with a smile like a grandmother scolding her grandson affectionately for some mischief, but with a latent malevolence in her expression that chilled me to the bone. I could see that all her teeth were made of steel, shining like tiny amber and silver fireflies in her macabre mouth.

Behind her, I noticed a second figure, semi-hidden in the shadows. It was one of our soldiers, perhaps German or Spanish. I identified him as one of ours by his stahlhelm helmet covered in a white tarp on his head. He was looking down with his arms hanging by his sides, completely unarmed and immobile, as if waiting for an order, standing a few meters behind the old woman.

I couldn't control the intense trembling in my hands and feet, which made me fall back as I tried to enter the cabin to warn García, because my voice had failed me. I finally stood up again, staggering through the room.

—G... Ga... García. Out... outside... the... the old lady, García. She's there... with... with a soldier.

—What old lady? Stop talking like that. Wait, did you say a soldier? —he said with a shocked voice, standing up from his chair with his rifle in hand. As if he hadn't heard his question, I added, stuttering...

—I... I think that... she's the owner of this place.

García approached the wall near the door, ready to shoot with his Mp40 at any moment. I heard the old woman's cracked voice speaking in Russian near the doorway. I didn't understand a single word, but there wasn't a trace of fear in her voice. Instead, she spoke to García as if addressing a child, without him understanding a word of Russian either.

He asked her menacingly about the unknown soldier accompanying her, what she had done to him, where she had found him, and what her intentions were. The old woman continued speaking in Russian, in her kindly yet sinister tone, perhaps trying to explain the situation to the armed corporal.

With no resolution due to the language barrier between the two, the atmosphere grew more and more tense. My trembling and breathing quickened. *Gallego*'s cried:

—She's here, she's here! —heightened the terror I felt.

I noticed the old woman's voice slowly took on a strange, guttural tone, and García's voice rose to the point of nearly shouting, his hands gripping the submachine gun tightly. Everything seemed to be leading to a violent climax, where I would hear a burst of gunfire against the old woman's body. Everything pointed to that violent outcome. Suddenly, the old woman snapped her fingers, and the sound cut through the darkness like a whip.

Gallego, who had been at the peak of his screaming, fainted onto the bed.

The dark figure of the soldier shuddered, as if he had been given an electric shock. Then a voice came from the shadows.

—The plague isn't red! —the slumped soldier slowly approached the doorway. He spoke Spanish quite well, but he slightly dragged his *'r'*, revealing an accent similar to German. Everything fell into a ghostly silence, broken only by the howling wind and the sound of the stranger's boots crunching through the snow as he approached. He stopped right in front of the first step of the stairs and, in the same position, spoke again, this time lower. —It isn't red. It's brown... and we're part of it. Isn't that right, Corporal García?

The addressed man lowered the weapon he had aimed at the two strangers, letting out a sigh of surprise.

—How do you know my name? Where do you know me from? Reveal your identity immediately, or I'll shoot you and the old woman too.

The soldier let out a mocking laugh and said...

—Really? Did it only take a day for you to forget me? I'm not surprised, Corporal. I hope your fingers haven't frozen any more, —he said, making a gesture as if he were slowly raising his tilted head, until his face appeared, half-smiling, looking with a certain arrogance at García.

I couldn't believe it. Even now, as I write, I refuse to think that this dull, mocking man was Walter. He seemed more like a copy, more dead than alive, of our fallen comrade. A poorly made caricature of the man who had once been our Walter. But there he was, in front of us, with the same face and the same insignia of our division on his uniform.

—You've got to be kidding me... No. It's impossible that it's you.

—Walter Braun von Juntz, my lord! Cadet of the Wehrmacht uniformed police! —he emphasized loudly, standing at attention and performing the official Hitler salute. He returned to his relaxed position and added sarcastically, —Hmm... yes, I think that's me.

The mysterious woman, who had faded into the background, let out a horrible cackle upon seeing him perform the Nazi salute mockingly.

—It's impossible that it's you...—García repeated, looking lost. —I saw the corpses of both of you. Yours and that hag's. You shouldn't even be here. Walter... I saw you die.

—You only saw me die?

—What do you mean by that? —I interjected, slightly relieved from my stupor.

—It's time, Juanma, for me to tell you a little story.

—No. It's time for me to tell it, —García interrupted, looking dryly at the soldier. I already knew he was hiding something, and that not-quite-dead Walter was about to speak the truth.

—I've heard your version already, —I said with double the dryness he had used on his interlocutor. —Who better than the victim himself to tell the story of his 'death'?

García relaxed his arms, lowering the gun in a gesture of resignation, and fell silent, giving in to Walter's affirmations.

—That day, I was terrified by the visions my fever was causing. At first, I didn't understand, and I was horrified by my fate. But now I'm part of something greater. —His eyes, sunken until they looked like two glassy pearls in the darkness of their sockets, took on a sudden gleam of joy. —The progeny of Magna Mater has chosen us, my friends. I am number six hundred and sixty-five of the chosen. I am the one who must reap the last angel.

When I fell into a deep sleep, my consciousness was taken to the center of the universe. And there it was. The magnificent Father of everything that exists. The one who was idioticized and confined by the Lord of the Great Abyss to the Infinite Void, where he sleeps forever, dreaming of our plane of reality, our known universe, our very existence, my friends.

It was like seeing God lulled by the rhythm of drums and flutes played by his formless angels. But the cycle is about to end. Azathoth needs more angels to play the melody that keeps him asleep. If he ever wakes up, it will be the end of everything that exists, and this dream in which we live, which sometimes seems like a nightmare, will end. Magna Mater is in charge of the harvest. We will save the universe.

We listened in astonishment to every word uttered by what had once been Walter but was now something else. His hands trembled with an inconceivable joy that manifested in his voice, driven by an unspeakable fanaticism.

It was as if he were speaking of a distorted version of the story told in the Holy Gospel. This Azathoth was his God, his Heavenly Father, calling him as a kind of Moses for the new era.

—When I awoke from my dream, the fever was gone, and I knew the truth. I knew my new purpose and mission in the universe, thanks to the revelations of the great Shub Niggurath. I saw you two, sleeping like children, my friends. I saw *Gallego* tossing in his sleep under his blankets, suffering from the pain and fever. I was going to free him from his misery. I would have transformed him into God's last flutist! —he exclaimed, raising his hand, trying to grasp something intangible in the air. Then he spoke with a mix of disdain and frustration, addressing García, clenching his fist as if whatever he had tried to grab had slipped away...

—But you had to intervene in my work, Corporal. You attacked me from behind when you saw me approaching *Gallego* and strangled me.

—You were insane! —García interrupted, startled. —What am I saying? You're insane! You were going to kill *Gallego*, you damned criminal.

—You prevented me from liberating him. He would have stopped suffering once and for all, but you didn't care about that. You don't care if people suffer. That's why you left me alone with him when we heard that explosion.

—I wouldn't let a sick man like you kill one of my men, you treacherous bastard. —García slowly raised his weapon again to prevent any reaction from Walter at that moment, who now turned to me...

—What are you waiting for? Teach this bastard a lesson. From the look on your face, I can see he gave you a beating, —he said, goading me maliciously. —Why don't you seek revenge? Break all his teeth and then avenge my 'death,' your friend Walter's death.

Now his voice came out with malice, slipping treacherously into my ears. In response, I grabbed my rifle and aimed it at that unrecognizable imitation of a human being.

—You're no longer our Walter. Don't try to confuse me. I won't let you kill *Gallego*, you cowardly wretch.

—So, I'm the traitor? I'm the coward? —he asked arrogantly. —We're on a sacred mission to prevent the end of all things, and you're trying to stop our work. You're turning your back on Creation itself! So, who's the traitor here?

—You are, —García snapped, now pointing the submachine gun at him. —You're crazier than the goat I just ate. The three of us are leaving now. We'll leave you and the old woman in your filthy hut with your witchcraft. You won't lay a finger on *Gallego*, and neither of you will be harmed.

Ignoring his terms, Walter began laughing as if it were a joke when he heard that García had eaten the goat.

—Tell me that's not true, Corporal. I recognize your bravery, really. It takes real guts to have swallowed Nug. Although you also must be very stupid.

—I ate your precious Nug. So what? What are you and the old hag going to do about it? Now, hands up.

—I think you misunderstand me, Corporal. Nug is the Great Father of the Sleeper of R'lyeh, the twin son of Shub Niggurath. The black goat you ate was only its vessel! It will try to break free from your belly at midnight, and you, without even meaning to, will become part of our work! —he proclaimed triumphantly, raising his arms, mockingly mimicking a gesture of surrender.

—Now are you telling me the goat was possessed? Look, we're leaving to hell with...

My focus shifted from Walter to García, who had interrupted his obscenity mid-sentence due to a violent stomach cramp. The old woman, who hadn't spoken another word until now, looked at the new moon in the clearing sky and, with an urgent smile, said something in Russian to Walter that sounded like

—*Vremya prishlo!* —after saying this, what unfolded before my eyes was something utterly maddening.

The woman shouted in a guttural voice in a language unfamiliar to me. Then, defying all the laws of physics, the old woman began to levitate to the height of our heads. After that, she disappeared in the blink of an eye, leaving behind the fleeting illusion similar to when you close your eyes and see, through your eyelids, the trace of the last image you observed. Walter, translating what the woman had said, declared...

—The time has come.

He approached García, who was now doubled over and writhing in excruciating stomach pain, forcing him to his knees.

—Stay away from him! —I shouted, aiming the gun at him. The rifle's sight wavered due to the terror making me tremble violently.

—After you strangled me, —Walter continued, despite obeying my warning and raising his arms in a gesture of surrender but not moving away from García, —Zhelezna, this servant of Magna Mater, unearthed me from the snow and brought me back to this world. That's why I owe this new life to her and to Shub Niggurath. I couldn't be happier, serving them and not you, you ungrateful corporal.

Poor García couldn't respond. The agonizing pain didn't even allow him to scream. Walter turned to me.

—I see our friend is still suffering, Juanma, —he said, tilting his head as if trying to see inside the house, where

Gallego lay unconscious. —Please, let me free him from his pain.

—I know very well what your way of freeing him will be. You made me think García had killed you, but all he was trying to do was save *Gallego* from you. Now I see who the real murderer is.

—Please, Juanma, you know me. You know I wouldn't kill a weak, innocent, injured man. You too can be part of our cause. You can redeem yourself from everything, just as I did. There's no greater honor than contributing to saving existence itself, and what better way than keeping the Great Sultan of Demons asleep forever? You saved my life back in Voljov when my squadron was being hit by waves of enemy soldiers, Juanma. You and your division of Spaniards rescued us. Now I offer you the chance to be part of the Great Cause. Can't you see? The four of us are together again. Let's become four more angels in Azathoth's Court.

—I'm sick of your stupid tales of angels and flutists, —I said, trembling with a mixture of confusion, anger, and fear. —You turned me against García and tried to kill *Gallego*, you crazy bastard. What's happening to García?... Where did the old witch go? How did she do that?

—Are you referring to the levitation? Ah... that's just an old spell. Teleportation is a bit more complicated, but there's no spell that Zhelezna can't perform. She's been touched by the great Shub Niggurath and has become a legend widely known throughout Eastern Europe for a long time. The peasants in the region know her as...

—Stop talking nonsense, —I interrupted, my finger on the trigger. I felt García, hunched on his elbows and knees, tug at my pants and vomit blood onto my boots. Then he looked up at me with pleading eyes.

All he could say was:

—Help me, Juanma, it's moving, —choking on something lodged in his throat. Horrified and furious, I turned to Walter. —Find the old woman and make her cure him!

—I'm sorry. There's nothing more we can do for him. But Nug must present himself at the Grand Mass, so...

He uttered the same words as the old woman, pointing the palm of his hand toward García. I watched in terror as my friend floated into the air and then vanished, just as the witch had.

—Where the hell... damn it, where did you take him?!

—He's with Zhelezna, at the Great Consecration, —he told me seriously. —You're invited too.

He gestured toward a dark path that disappeared into the forest. Before I could regain my fear, I struck him on the head with the butt of my rifle. He fell into the snow, and before he could react, I managed to tie his hands behind his back to one of the "legs" of the house.

That way, he wouldn't be able to try anything against *Gallego* while I ventured into that narrow path through the thick forest to go after poor García. It was my duty as a soldier and as a man to rescue him from wherever he was, to help him heal, and, above all, to ask for his forgiveness. I had no choice. All I hoped was that Walter wouldn't wake up or somehow free himself before I returned, or a tragedy could occur with *Gallego* at the hands of that madman.

I armed myself with the MP40 that García had dropped before disappearing and ran, stumbling through the fresh snow, down the dark stretch between the trees. As I got closer, I could hear a strange murmuring, like praises. A breeze brushed my face, bringing a sharp, unfamiliar smell to my nose.

I reached the end of the path. It wasn't exactly a clearing, but the trees were more spread out in a dip in the terrain. Before getting closer, I had to crouch down behind a large fallen trunk at the edge of the slope to observe, without being discovered, the Dantean scene unfolding before me.

A crowd of people of various ages, from children to the elderly, men and women alike, stood singing monotonously in an unknown language, forming a circle around a bonfire.

Through binoculars, I saw a silhouette outlined against the firelight, and I quickly identified it as García. He was writhing in pain.

I was ready to burst into the crowd, shooting, but before I descended the small slope, I observed something terrifying and bewildering that paralyzed my muscles.

Not everyone present was human. They only appeared to be. They were pale figures, devoid of any clothing or fur. They were short in stature and mimicked apes in certain movements. They also had canine features on their faces and long, pointed ears.

To one side, above the central bonfire, floated that repulsive old woman.

I saw the swollen image of García rise again to the same height as the old woman. The noise from the sinister crowd grew louder when, before my terrified eyes, García's body exploded like a grenade.

My God. The goat really contained something aberrant inside it. García had foolishly eaten it, and now that thing had been released from within his body.

García no longer existed. I would never be able to ask for his forgiveness for blaming him for Walter's false death. I felt guilt and overwhelming terror. The kind of terror that can make even the toughest man cry in fear overcame me as I watched that amorphous, gigantic thing that completely destroyed García from the inside.

The creature was a formless mass, a black jelly filled with tentacles, protrusions, and mouths from which strings of saliva dripped. The putrid smell it emitted was like dog breath and rotting meat, so strong that it made me vomit.

The cries of the crazed mob bubbled with joy and profane praises. The uproar reached its peak when the witch's body also exploded.

The witch's essence dissipated into the night air with a scream, a mixture of agony and jubilation, uttering some kind of spell in an unknown language. It seemed that the woman also harbored something infinitely abhorrent inside her, just like the black goat, and now an exact copy of the thing that killed García was appearing.

Two twin abominations floated, groaning horribly and regurgitating under the light of the bonfire, around which the horde of beings, crazed by their own chants and cries, repeated,

—Ïa ïa ïa Shub Niggurath...

The pinnacle of absolute horror came afterward when a cloud of such intense blackness, like coal smoke, heavy with an air of extreme malice, began to descend over the place, above the two repugnant things. It seemed to respond to the maddening call of its servants, like an intelligence beyond human comprehension.

Then the smoky shadow manifested in a horrifying material form. The entity looked like the other two deformities beneath it, but much larger. Thank heaven that the darkness of the night and the height at which it hovered above the bonfire didn't allow me to clearly make out its appearance. What horrible fate would have awaited me if I had dared to charge in down there? God forbid I even imagine it.

That monstrosity was far worse than its two miniatures. Its jaws emitted a sound unlike anything I'd ever heard before. Countless tentacles and black goat legs appeared from its lower part. Sometimes, small creatures were born from it, which the mass quickly swallowed up again after they fell, while others managed to escape. Perhaps one of those was the thing that bit Walter.

Had I seen that gigantic, nebulous aberration in full clarity, I wouldn't hesitate for a second to tear out my own eyes, never to witness anything so monstrous again. So... was that inter-cosmic abomination Shub Niggurath? The famous Magna Mater of the dark offspring?

Fortunately, my urge to flee from that place outweighed my desire to empty my entire machine gun magazine on those aberrations. Who knows what fate awaited me if I had attacked the horde, Shub Niggurath, and her twins. I got up and rushed back to the cabin.

I didn't manage to rescue poor García, and guilt and fear ate away at me from the inside. Going to that infernal place was a colossal waste of time. I had accomplished nothing. There was nothing I could do.

I didn't stop running for even a second on my way back, never looking over my shoulder. Finally, I made it back to the clearing by the cabin.

With horror, I saw a pile of cut ropes next to the pillar where I had left what had once been Walter tied up. The living dead had freed himself.

I quickly ran up the stairs and entered the cabin. I arrived just in time. Walter, with a bayonet in his hand, was staggering across the room. He was heading toward where *Gallego* lay unconscious on the floor, in front of the cabinet filled with strange objects and rare books.

My machine gun was loaded, and I instantly aimed it at the undead. The being that had been Walter didn't even seem to notice my sudden arrival.

—Don't you dare touch him, —I ordered, panting in the darkness.

—You saw us, didn't you? —he said without turning, in a voice that sounded like two people speaking at once, which I found extremely disturbing. —Wasn't it beautiful?

—I saw what they did to García, you bastard.

—No. He did that to himself. No one forced him to eat the goat, which housed my brother Nug.

—Your brother? Look, all of you are out of your minds. That thing... Shub Niggurath. How can you serve a monster like that?

—You know, —he sighed and started speaking about himself in the third person, —before this boy joined the army, he studied at the most prestigious academy in his nation. His father was quite wealthy, so he could afford that luxury. His father wanted him to study the different languages of the continent, especially the one you speak. At first, he hated your language. He found it the most complicated of them all and, for that reason, disliked it. But then, forced by his father; after studying the language in depth, he understood it. That's how it became, of all the languages, Walter's favorite. He realized how beautiful your language is, Juanma, one of the richest in humanity. So many accents, so many verb forms.

—What's your point with this story? And why are you talking like that? —I interrupted him.

—Humans see the unpleasantness in things they don't understand. They don't care if it's good or bad. Anything that goes beyond what's considered normal is rejected, hated, and feared. That's how ignorant your species is.

His voice turned resentful and threatening, almost like a growl. He slowly turned toward me. I could see his pale face and completely white eyes. I understood from his spasms, his erratic movements, and especially the way he spoke in the third person that what was speaking to me wasn't Walter. That thing was a puppet of flesh and bone, controlled at will by the terrible Yeb, the horrendous twin brother of Nug who had once resided in the witch's body, communicating with me.

—We offered you a new beginning, and you rejected it. Corporal García brought about his own fate, and we are to blame in your eyes. And when we tried to save this poor soul, he stopped me and wanted to end Walter's life. You're incapable of understanding that beyond this earthly life of suffering, there's something worth it, Juanma. The salvation of the universe. We must prevent Azathoth from waking up and...

—I'm sick of all this! Enough of your talk of those things, you, disgusting abomination! You'll never convince me that any of this is normal! Just let us leave this place and leave my friend's body alone, damn it!

But the monster ignored my outburst of impatience and continued with its macabre speech, turning toward *Gallego* a gain...

—Finally, I can free your soul, *Gallego*! Nothing will stop you from becoming the last angel tonight, under the new moon of the forest! Here, in the cold darkness of the taiga, in the name of Shub Niggurath, I release your soul from the prison of material flesh!

He howled hoarsely as I watched, alarmed, as he raised the bayonet, intending to plunge it into the still-unconscious *Gallego*'s body. At that moment, I squeezed the trigger of the MP40 with all my strength.

The burst of gunfire tore into Walter's back. The flashes illuminated the small room for a few seconds. A chilling scream emerged from the riddled body that didn't seem to come from him. The smell of gunpowder filled the room, along with a rush of foul, cold air that smelled exactly like the place where those horrible things had appeared. At the same time, I felt cold blood splatter my face. I heard the body fall heavily to the ground.

I should have felt sadness and pity for the man lying there in the darkness, but that thing writhing spasmodically on the floor had ceased to be my friend Walter many hours ago.

Without wasting time, I rushed to *Gallego*, wondering how he had gotten off the bed and made his way to the front of the cabinet. But from the darkness, like a bolt of lightning, Walter's riddled body rose and crashed hard into me, knocking me onto my back.

He no longer spoke but emitted hoarse growls like a rabid dog. Struggling on top of me, he tried to bite my face. He was like an animal driven by the sole urge to kill, scratching and drooling like a wild beast. He pinned me to the ground, bringing his gnashing jaws closer to my face. I couldn't feel his breath. He didn't have any.

I grabbed him by the collar of his coat and threw him forcefully to the side, managing to knock him onto his back to my right. When I tried to fire another burst, the gun jammed, so I reached for my pistol. But before I could grab it, the living dead lunged forward and grabbed my leg. I stifled a scream of pain when his teeth sank into my calf.

Seeing that despite my thrashing, I couldn't shake him off, I resorted to shooting him in the head with the pistol. Three times! I shot him three times in the skull, yet he still moved on the ground, convulsing with a face that stirred deep compassion!

—Goodbye, Walter, —I said with a tear in my eye before stomping on the head of what had once been my great friend and comrade, just yesterday.

Before getting ready to carry *Gallego* out as quickly as possible, I sat next to Walter's corpse for a long time, crying as my mind screamed for release. All the terror, guilt, and grief crystallized at that moment, alongside *Gallego*, who was beginning to wake up.

I wiped the tears from my face and prepared to lift the wounded man onto my shoulder to get out of there. Then I heard the noise of those things praising Shub Niggurath in that small valley... There was no doubt they were approaching. Perhaps Yeb was using them as a last resort to claim his final two sacrifices.

With my last bit of strength, I'm writing these lines in my diary. My leg hurts a lot from the bite.

I hear Yeb's voice inside my head. He's talking to me. Now I know what my friends saw and heard. I'm feeling strange impulses I've never felt before.

They want me. They want me to give them the *Gallego*'s life.

The crowd is out there. They surround the house. They want us to become the last deformed angels of Azathoth, the Idiot Chaos.

But I won't allow it. I'll fight until my last breath.

They're trying to force the door, but the barricade I improvised with the cuckoo clock, the old cabinet full of strange objects, and the rest of the furniture is holding up well.

I hear screams and crashes outside. I can't even tell anymore if they're real or just hallucinations.

My weapon is ready. When the door gives in, it'll be my bullets that fly through this damned taiga...

I still don't know whether it was fortune or misfortune that I, Mateo Gonzalo Sánchez, also known as *Gallego*, the idiot who lost the MG42 and got shot while taking a piss, was injured and unconscious the whole time. I would have helped them and wouldn't have been a complete burden along their journey.

I tried to warn them, gripped by the terrible visions that shook my sanity in those desolate places. Poor Walter had tried as well. I attempted to save García from the horrible death that awaited him for eating Nug's vessel, by offering him a quicker and more merciful death. But I don't blame them for not listening to me.

Any normal human being, in their eternal skepticism, would never think that a supernatural entity and all its servants were pursuing them. A regular person would have assumed my shouts of warning were the product of the fever driving me mad.

Despite my condition, I knew very well what was happening around me and was aware of these malevolent beings thanks to my grandfather, who knew much about these matters. In his younger years, he had intensely studied the occult sciences alongside his profession as an archaeologist.

Once, he even had the opportunity to travel to the United States. He established good relations with scholars at

Miskatonic University, in a quaint New England town. Due to his credentials, they granted him access to the infamous Necronomicon, written by the mad Arab Abdul Alhazred, which the university kept locked away in a vault.

In the pages of that infamous book, there are accounts of creatures that descended from the stars to Earth long before all known life appeared. Among them was Cthulhu, the Dreamer of R'lyeh, a horror that fell from the cosmos and lay in an underwater prison in the middle of the ocean.

This monstrosity was spawned by none other than Nug, the same abomination who, alongside Yeb, both worshiped by ghouls and the sect of Abboth, were known as the blasphemous twins, the rotten progeny of the Magna Mater, the Black Goat of the Woods with a Thousand Young.

No human, without proper preparation, deserves the misfortune of witnessing these entities. I feel immense pity for Juanma, who, despite all his bravery, ended up dying at the hands of the Russians.

Some troops, camped relatively nearby, had heard the sound of gunfire and came to that cursed clearing. They were immediately attacked by those horrible creatures, but they eliminated them with sheer firepower and grenades.

They found my Cuban friend, rifle in hand, blindly defending the entrance to the cabin. Since he refused to surrender, they shot him down.

They found me unconscious, with this diary in the pocket of my coat.

In a way, Juanma saved me again because, not knowing the Spanish language, the Russians forced me to translate and transcribe the text of the manuscript so many times that I've memorized it. I think they haven't killed me because they expect me to explain what happened there.

I will always be eternally grateful to them for saving my life more than once. To him, to García, and to Walter, before he became a servant of Shub Niggurath.

As for the Grand Harvest of Angels to save the entire universe and existence itself, the mission that the undead Walter fervently proclaimed, I want to believe it was nothing more than a deception by Shub Niggurath to devour the souls of the servants forever.

The Necronomicon states that those amorphous flutists who lull Azathoth, the Nuclear Chaos of the Universe, have never and will never follow any cycle in which they are relieved of their duties.

Those are eternal entities that need nothing more than to keep the Demon Sultan asleep forever. They never tire or die. And while the infamous Necronomicon predicts the eventual awakening of Azathoth, absolutely no one knows when that day will come.

It is said that neither Shub Niggurath nor any of the Outer Gods care in the slightest about our insignificant existence in the universe, and that we have the bad habit of believing we are the center of everything.

But one thing has haunted my thoughts since that fateful night in the cursed cabin lost in the heart of the taiga.

After I woke from my delirium, completely alone in that place, I untied myself from the cot and walked over to the horrible cabinet filled with witchcraft and ancient books.

My hand, almost moving on its own, reached for one of the old tomes and opened it to a fateful page, the contents of which caused me to faint again.

There, at the end of a list with six hundred and sixty-six entries written in archaic characters, were the names of my three friends... and my own.

UNDER THE ALGOL´S SHINE

—Are you sure you know what you're doing?

—Of course, Reinier, I did this a million times during the boarding school to sneak into the girls' dorm. Even on nights much darker than this, —I replied as I removed another slat from the shutter. —Just hold on a bit longer, and don't worry, no one usually comes around here. Well, except for the new guard. They don't call him Burned Man for nothing.

Despite being tall and skinny as a bamboo shoot, my friend Reinier held me firmly on his shoulders so I could reach the small, high window on the wall of The Heel. It was a moonless night, but the clear skies glow allowed me to work without needing extra light to accomplish the task that would let us access the secluded building.

In the architectural salad of styles that make up Central University, The Heel stood out for its appearance and unique location. No one knew for sure what the original purpose of this tower was, located at the farthest edge of the expansive square that was our Alma Mater. Theories ranged from a base for a telescope to a site for installing an ENIAC computer to the wildest rumor that it was a chapel dedicated to a dark cult of pagan gods of hidden knowledge.

The three-story concrete structure, with an exterior profile made up of four walls, one concave and the opposite convex, earned the nickname "The Heel" because one of the more outlandish legends about its origin claimed it was part of an abandoned project celebrating the revolution. The architectural ensemble was supposed to be a gigantic sculpture in the shape of a military boot, of which the building would obviously be the heel.

What everyone agreed on was that no one had ever seen the door in the concave wall or the three modest windows in the convex wall open. Its current function was also a complete mystery.

For several days, I had felt the dubious pride of belonging to the select group that not only had seen the door of The Heel open but had been inside and knew its function.

As part of the fifteen days of mandatory volunteer work required of all students to meet the internal needs of the University, I had been assigned to work in The Heel. With some disappointment, I discovered that the institution used the mysterious place simply as a storage room for the oldest bound theses and the least-used books from the library's collection.

Those dusty materials that filled the sturdy metal shelves were being slowly digitized, so my task was to methodically remove them from their place, box them, and transport them to the computing center, where they would be scanned, transferring their information from archaic cellulose to modern bits stored in databases. My job was to use my muscles to move the loads.

The first few days of work, after the initial curiosity faded, were a mix of tedium and the unpleasant realization that one day, my thesis, on which I was working so diligently, would end up in that pile of moth food.

It seemed the rest of the period would be that same monotony until one day, the University employee overseeing the work asked me to move a shelf in front of the back wall of the ground floor. Thinking the thing must weigh a ton, I applied considerable force, and to my surprise, the massive shelf slid smoothly on small hidden rails in the floor. Behind it was a sturdy steel door.

The boss opened a panel hidden in the wall and took out an ancient-looking key to unlock the newly revealed door.

—Let's go, today the work is in the basement, —he said in his usual indifferent tone as he flipped a switch. A row of old incandescent lamps cast a weak yellow light on the space beyond the door.

That day, I discovered that The Heel had five floors underground, accessible via a black-painted steel spiral staircase. In that place rested even less-used documents, escaping total oblivion thanks to a lucky reference in the dark files of the library.

When we reached the fifth level, the air was stale and dusty. Our boss flipped another switch, and some ventilation system behind the concrete walls started working, making the atmosphere tolerable within a few minutes.

The content on the shelves there was a bit different. These were books with heavy leather covers, with titles embossed in silver or gold lettering.

—Is this some alchemist's library? —one of my workmates joked.

—More or less, —the employee replied seriously. —This collection was added to the University's many decades ago and was found in the abandoned mansion of an old family from the city.

To everyone's surprise, the man's usual indifferent tone had given way to unexpected nostalgia.

—Rumor had it that they practiced the occult, with human sacrifices and all sorts of witchcraft. When the neighbors reported that they hadn't seen the last heir, who lived alone in the decaying mansion, for about two months, the police broke the locks and entered. They found no trace of the old man, so they assumed he had left the country illegally, and all the property passed to the State.

The man approached one of the shelves and took one of the ancient volumes. He opened it and leafed through its yellowed pages.

—My grandfather used to tell me, —he continued, —that the whole story became an urban legend for a while, but today, everyone's forgotten about it. The only things left are these books, saved because someone found them valuable for their appearance. They probably had no idea of their contents.

A heavy silence reigned, intensified by the hum of the hidden fans. At that moment, I was overcome by an inexplicable sense of loss, as if something I wasn't fully aware belonged to me had been violently ripped away, absorbed into an alien, unknown dimension. I looked at my companions, and they all seemed to feel the same way.

The spell was suddenly broken by the sound of the book snapping shut in our boss's hand. He returned the volume to its place and said in his usual tone.

—Today's work is to take these batches to the Computing Center, so let's go. We don't have all eternity.

That day, the work was grueling. Climbing the spiral staircase while carrying heavy boxes quickly lost its appeal after the first trip. Especially when the shadows cast by the old lamps danced mockingly, confusing your senses and making you lose sight of the small triangular steps.

In fact, one of my colleagues missed a step and tumbled down the spiral, followed by a cascade of destroyed boxes, old heavy books, and the remnants of the broken transport crates. His body slammed into one of the shelves, knocking several volumes loose, adding to the chaos.

—Please, be careful! —our boss shouted. —You, help him up. The rest of you, pick up the books from the floor.

I was one of those tasked with gathering the scattered books. It was there, crouched in that basement, surrounded by dusty pages and forgotten knowledge, that I saw it for the first time.

It was in front of me, open on the floor to some random page. Its worn yellow leather cover seemed to stare directly at me, inviting me to read its contents. There lay the cursed book that had caused so much misfortune. The large golden letters seemed to glow, forming its title: "*Viarium quae Carcosa*".

As if in a trance, I slowly reached out to grab it and read its pages, but the university employee's hand was quicker.

The man picked up the volume and snapped it shut. With precise movements, he placed it on the highest shelf and scolded me.

—Get up, there's still a lot of work to do, and I don't want any more delays.

That day, we transported the contents of several shelves, but we didn't get to the shelf where the yellow-covered book lay. The next day, the task was on the third floor. When I asked the boss if we were going to continue working in the basement, he responded with his apathetic tone,

—We have other priorities now.

The next day, while we were in the university dining hall, facing the questionable squid in sauce that passed for dinner's main course, I was recounting the curious event to my tablemates when I heard a familiar voice behind me, one I hadn't heard in many years, asking,

—Are you sure that was the title?

—Well, I don't speak Latin as well as you, —I replied, standing up, —but I'm sure that's what was written on the cover, Reinier.

I turned around, and there, holding a tray of food, was my old friend. His face was a bit more haggard than I remembered, and he was much taller and thinner, but the smile and eyes were the same as always.

—Make room at the table for the most cultured and intelligent person I know.

—Don't exaggerate, —Reinier replied as he sat down, —but if what you're saying is true, then you really need to meet more people.

Reinier and I were born in the same small town, lost deep in the province. For as long as I could remember, we played together, whether among the massive parts taken from the sugar mill when it wasn't running or staring at the stars, lying on our backs in the sugarcane-filled railcars parked in the rail yard before the locomotives carried their loads to the tipper.

Being with Reinier was always a fun adventure. Thanks to his fertile imagination, any giant piece of metal became a spaceship traveling through the galaxy.

Even as a child, my friend could identify the constellations in the sky and, while we chewed on chunks of sugarcane, he would tell me the legends associated with each of them. The fuel for those ideas came from the knowledge passed down by his grandfather and the vast, well-stocked library they had in their home, one of the largest in our town, since Reinier's family was considered old money, as they said around here.

Despite the slight eccentric reputation of his family and my own humble origins, our friendship had always been strong. It only cooled when Reinier went off to study at the Vocational School in the provincial capital, while I went to the pre-university school, lost among the endless fields of the interior plains.

Since our weekend leave never coincided, we stopped seeing each other. Back then, we didn't have the communication options we have today, so we completely lost contact.

The only vague news I'd heard about him was that during his military service, he had suffered a terrible accident, and afterward, he began studying Geology at a distant province's university.

Now we were together again, laughing as we devoured the terrible squid in sauce.

After dinner, I invited him to my dorm room to catch up and have some drinks from my stash of ninety-proof alcohol, watered down with tap water and "aged" with shards of oak barrel wood that a friend had gotten from a rum factory. Reinier accepted the invitation but warned me that he didn't drink alcohol.

That night, we took advantage of access to the roof of the dorm building. Lying on our backs, staring at the starry sky, we shared stories of what had happened during our time apart.

Reinier explained that just a month ago, he had managed to transfer to Central University. Thanks to his excellent grades, he'd pulled off the miracle of switching from Geology to Architecture.

—At least I'm closer to home, —he said. —Since the accident, the old man worries about me too much.

—By the way, I heard rumors about that. Was it really that bad?

My friend sat up; his gaze lost in the void. With his right hand, he held something hanging from his neck, inside his shirt.

—It was... transformative. We were doing military service at a base high on a hill, deep in the woods. Two comrades and I went out to hunt hutias to supplement our food, and we ended up falling into a sinkhole. We were lost in the dark for several days...

I sat up as well. I had heard about that incident when I was also doing military service. Three recruits had fallen into a sinkhole. They were found almost by miracle, several days later. One of them didn't survive; the other two were taken to the hospital in critical condition.

Inexplicably, a few days later, one of them escaped from the intensive care unit and threw himself in front of a train. The other was in a coma for almost a month. I had never imagined that my dear friend Reinier was one of the victims of that disaster.

Returning to normal, my friend looked up at the stars again and casually commented,

—So, what's this story about the yellow-covered book?

I told him about the incident in the basement of The Heel, including the parts I had left out in previous accounts meant for a wider audience. That is, I spoke of the strange sensations I had felt under the influence of those old tomes.

When I finished the story, my friend stared at me with a strange expression for a few moments. Then he lay back down on the hard concrete of the roof. He raised an arm, pointing with a long, slender finger at the clear sky.

—Do you see that bright star in the constellation of Perseus? Its name is Algol, which comes from the Arabic *Ras al-Ghul*, meaning 'the head of the demon.' The ancient sages noticed that the star's brightness changed periodically, and they considered it an aberration of the natural laws, the work of the devil. Today we know it's actually a system of three stars, and its intensity depends on their alignment.

Reinier sat up again, gripping what he had around his neck beneath his shirt, and commented,

—It's strange how things align in the chaotic dance of destiny.

I sat up too and observed my friend, who lowered his eyes from the sky and looked at me with a smile.

—Do you think you could help me sneak into that building and take a look at the yellow-covered book?

And that's how we found ourselves in this situation, with me finishing the removal of the slats from the shutter while perched on my friend's bony shoulders.

—Done, —I said. —I think this will be enough...

—Are you sure no one ever comes around here? —Reinier asked, —because someone with a flashlight just appeared on the path, and it looks like they're heading this way.

—It must be that paranoid nut, Burned Man, —I grumbled. —We need to hurry.

I quickly climbed through the window. From my time working inside The Heel, I remembered that below the window was a shelf full of old theses. The worn bindings held my weight without issue. I pulled my friend up by his backpack. He climbed, kicking against the wall without much grace.

I hurriedly replaced the slats in their original position. I finished just in time as the beam of the guard's flashlight swept across the closed window.

—Is someone there? —came the neurotic voice of Burned Man. —I know you're here, counter-revolutionary worms. Don't think I'll let you sabotage and damage State property!

My friend and I even held our breath as the light filtered under the door, swaying as the stubborn guard tried to open it. However, the old lock held firm. After a while, we heard Burned Man walking away, shouting:

—Don't think you've fooled me, despicable worms. I know you're in there! I won't let you get away with this!

When the noises faded into the night, we descended and headed to the movable shelf. The mechanism slid smoothly on its rails, revealing the metal door. Confidently, I opened the panel to retrieve the key, and that's when I had the first unpleasant surprise of the night. The niche was empty.

—The key was here...

—Let me see, —Reinier said as he pulled out a lockpick from his pocket and began working on the lock.

—But since when...—I began to say in surprise, but the sound of the door opening interrupted me.

—The switch is around here, right? —Reinier said, feeling along the wall until he activated the mechanism.

At night, the light from the lamps seemed more intense.

—Hurry, that glow can be seen from outside, —my friend urged me as he closed the door behind us. —For obvious reasons, we can't turn on the fan, so be prepared for the stale air.

I descended the steps like an automaton, trying to understand how my friend, whom I'd known since childhood, was behaving this way and moving with such familiarity in that environment, not like someone descending the torturous stairs for the first time into an entirely unknown place.

—Which shelf was the book on? —he asked when we reached the fifth level.

Still dazed, I pointed with my finger, but where I indicated was only an empty space. Reinier frowned darkly and shook his head as he clutched again the object hanging from his neck.

—Hmm, close. It's here. I can feel it...

—Reinier, can you explain what's going on?

Without answering, my friend pulled out what he had been keeping inside his shirt. It was a strange teardrop-shaped stone, with a hole through which a small chain passed, allowing him to wear it around his neck. Across the smooth surface of the object, a yellow symbol glowed with varying intensity, depending on how close Reinier brought it to the books on the shelves. After a brief search, when he approached the last level of the most distant shelf, the thing glowed like a small star.

—So, this is where they hid you, huh? —my friend almost shouted with a voice strange and completely unfamiliar to me.

With incredible agility, Reinier scaled the shelf and removed some volumes from the top level until he found what he was looking for. He slowly descended, now with equally precise movements. Ignoring me completely, he muttered under his breath while flipping through the book, its leather cover shining with the title *Viarium quae Carcosa*.

—Ever since you sent me the first clue, in that hellish pit, I've followed your instructions. The others were weak, or they lacked the intelligence to decipher your riddles, but I am strong and cunning. I deserve to find the end of the secret paths. I deserve to reach Carcosa and quench my thirst for knowledge in its eternal halls.

—But what are you talking about, Reinier? —I shouted at him.

His face, illuminated from below by the supernatural glow of the stone hanging from his neck, was a mask of demonic ecstasy, with the expression of a hunter who, after a long and tortuous chase, was about to catch his prey. I grabbed him by the shoulders and shook him, forcing him to close the cursed book.

The yellowish eyes that glared at me with infinite fury were not my friend's.

At that moment, the metallic sound of the lock on the basement door echoed. Burned Man's psychotic voice filled the space.

—See? I was right, comrade. The light is on. This is the work of counter-revolutionary saboteur worms.

—Calm down, Godinez, —the apathetic voice replied. I immediately recognized as belonging to the University employee who had been my boss these past few days. —Maybe someone just forgot to turn off the lights after finishing work. Either way, let's check each floor, just to put your mind at ease.

The metal steps began to clatter under the weight of the two men descending the stairs. Suddenly, an irrational panic clouded my mind completely. How had I let myself get dragged into a situation like this? Cornered like a rat in that dusty hole. The person I considered my best friend was clearly insane, perhaps traumatized by the terrible experience he'd endured in that sinkhole, and his mind was lost in some delusion that could only lead us to disaster.

—The next level is the last, —I heard the University employee say, but his apathetic tone turned to concern with his next words. —But, Godinez, where did you get that gun?

The unmistakable sound of a pistol's slide chambering a round exponentially increased the panic I was feeling.

—I'm going to shower those counter-revolutionary saboteur worms with lead, —shouted Burned Man. —Do you hear me, filthy rats? You'll regret attacking the Revolution!

I was trembling, not knowing what to do, when a firm hand rested on my shoulder. I turned instinctively and nearly screamed in terror. Reinier was holding a strange black, curved dagger in his right hand, a smile on his lips.

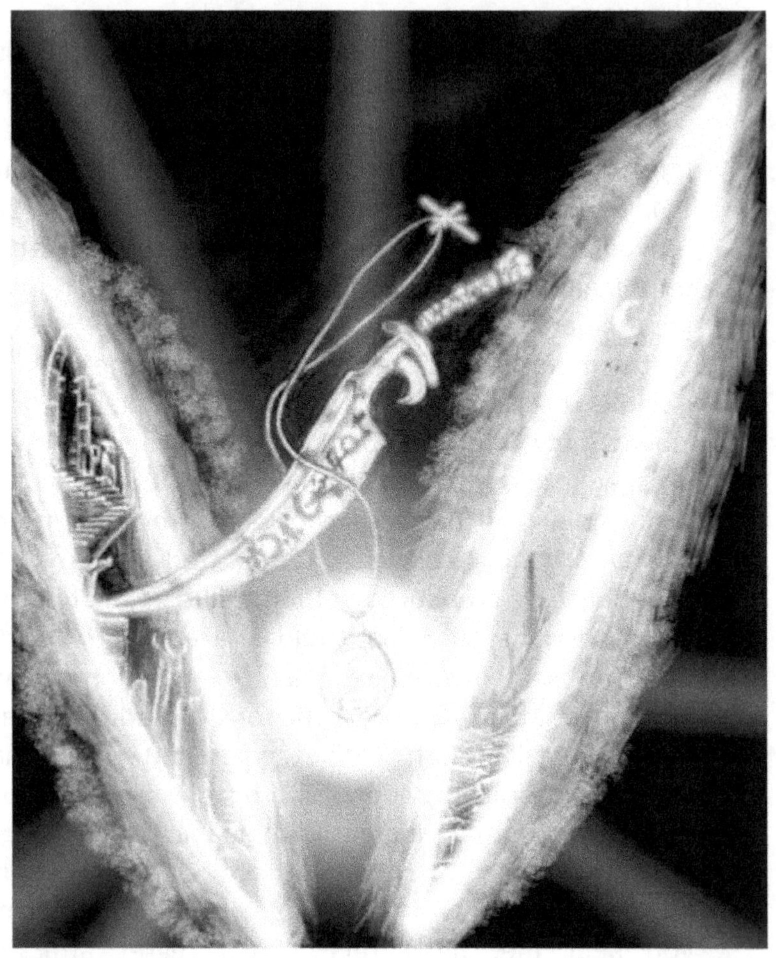

To my surprise, the very fabric of space-time gave way under the supernatural edge, and two transverse cuts opened in the structure of reality. One was dark, but from the other, a yellowish glow seeped through.

—This is the end for me, —I thought, but when I looked into my friend's eyes, I recognized the expression I knew so well. It wasn't the look of a madman or a killer, —it was the look of triumph.

With a swift motion, Reinier made a small cut on the tip of his index finger and used his blood to draw a series of strange symbols on the black blade. Then he made two slashes in the air, side by side.

To my surprise, the very fabric of space-time gave way under the supernatural edge, and two transverse cuts opened in the structure of reality. One was dark, but from the other, a yellowish glow seeped through.

I took a deep breath to ask something, but before I could say anything, Reinier winked at me and nodded as if to say, "Don't worry, everything will be fine", and pushed me toward the dark slit. The last thing I remember is seeing him step through the other preternatural opening and disappear into the yellow glow.

When I regained consciousness, I felt like I was lying on an uneven, uncomfortable surface. I opened my eyes and saw a starry sky where Algol shone its light upon me. The sounds reaching my ears were intimately familiar. I sat up and realized I was atop a sugarcane-filled railcar in the yard of my hometown's railway.

My family was very surprised when I knocked on the door of our house at such an unexpected hour, but they welcomed me with their usual joy.

The next morning, they informed me that Reinier's grandfather had passed away a few days earlier, and curiously, he had left a sealed envelope for me.

When I had enough privacy, I broke the seal and checked the contents. Inside was just a small, folded paper. On it, written in an old-fashioned, ornate handwriting, were the words:

"Please, find Reinier."

When I returned to the University, there was a frenzy of activity. A fire had completely destroyed the contents of The Heel.

According to the official version, someone had left the basement lights on, and when two employees went to turn them off, a spark had caused an explosion in the building's stale air. A guard named Godinez had died instantly, and another University employee was seriously injured but out of danger.

No one knows anything about my friend Reinier. It's as if he had been erased from our plane of existence. Considering his family has no known relatives, all his properties will pass to the State.

As for me, I can't explain what happened that night, and I haven't spoken to anyone about it. I'm having trouble sleeping, and I often dream of a strange city, full of absurdly tall buildings with eccentric and impossible structures under a sky where yellow lights dance chaotically, like an alienating eternal aurora borealis. In one of the lost halls of that labyrinthine place, my dear friend Reinier smiles as he avidly reads from endless tomes.

I hadn't worried about my situation until a few days ago, when, back in my regular University classes, I found myself unconsciously drawing a strange symbol in my notebook. The same symbol embedded in the small teardrop-shaped stone with a hole through which passes a silver chain, allowing me to wear it around my neck. I had found it in my pocket when I woke up atop the sugarcane railcar, bathed in the light of Algol.

Now I'm a little worried because I feel an intense urge for understand everything. A burning desire to find hidden clues. An uncontrollable thirst for knowledge.

CHARYBDIS

—So, you don't know anything about this thing either? —Andrei asked.

—Knowing is a complicated term, my friend, —the elderly antique dealer replied with a heavy Galician accent, looking over the top of his glasses at the customer.

His tanned skin, good physical condition, and meticulously tousled hair might have given the false impression that the man was much younger, but the sharp perception of the old man wasn't easily deceived.

—None of the antique dealers in the city could give me any information about this statuette, —the man said with a hint of disappointment in his voice, —but they all recommended that I come to you, as you have a reputation for being an expert on the most unusual objects. I came last because your shop is quite far, though I must admit, it's quite picturesque.

Andrei smiled politely, standing in front of the counter where he had placed the enigmatic statuette with its iridescent cord. The shop was filled with a wide variety of strange, ancient-looking artifacts, along with numerous books bound in old leather with gold or silver titles.

The old man leaned over the object to inspect it with a small magnifying glass that hung around his neck.

—For example, I know that the statuette itself is carved from a rather valuable variety of white marble, —the antique dealer muttered. —It represents the bust of a robust man with curly hair and two grapevines on either side of his head. Although it looks Greco-Roman, it's much older than those civilizations. The cord that comes with it seems to be...

The old man straightened up, his expression growing clouded with concern.

—Where and when did you find this object, my friend? —he asked.

—I like walking along the beach early in the morning after stormy nights, —Andrei explained. —The tide usually brings interesting things, and last night's storm was quite intense, —lightning and thunder like I've never seen before. It felt like something from another world...

—In fact, it seemed like something from another world, —the old man agreed pensively.

—Well, I found that thing this morning, —Andrei continued. —It was half-buried in the sand. The strangest part is that the cord got caught between my toes. It's almost like I was meant to find it.

The antique dealer observed Andrei closely with an inscrutable expression on his face. Leaving the piece on the counter, he hobbled over to a cabinet at the far end of the shop, retrieving a few objects from one of the drawers and slipping them into the pockets of his vest.

—Sciatica acting up? —Andrei asked, trying to make small talk as he curiously eyed a thick book on the counter.

The book stood out from the rest of the shop's atmosphere as it was a more recent publication. Andrei read the shiny cover in his mind: *"Tachyonic Storms and Wormholes: Viable Methods for Time Travel?"*

—A lingering wound from the war, —the antique dealer replied as he donned a pair of fine black suede gloves with strange silver symbols on the back.

With his hands properly gloved, the old man took the magnifying glass from his vest pocket that he had retrieved earlier from the cabinet. It was a large object made of coppery metal covered in strange symbols. The lens itself was thick and had a greenish tint.

—Sometimes we find things, my friend, —he said while studying the statuette with the peculiar magnifying glass. —Other times, things find us.

The old man straightened up, sighing deeply, his posture stiff and his gaze unreadable to Andrei.

—What's your name, my friend? —the old man asked, putting the magnifying glass back into his vest pocket.

—You can call me Andrei.

—Well, Andrei, I'm sorry I can't help you more at this time. I truly am.

Andrei picked up the statuette from the counter, a bit irritated. He felt like he had wasted his time. He was about to leave the shop when the old man called out to him again.

—Please, take this, —the antique dealer said, extending his trembling hand with what looked like a business card between his fingers. —It might be useful when things get very difficult.

Andrei slipped the small card into his pocket and hung the mysterious statuette around his neck.

"At least it's a nice ornament" Andrei thought. He put on his sunglasses over his honey-colored eyes and left the shop.

He headed to his job in the city center, resigned to leaving the origin of the strange object as a mystery.

For a moment, he thought he saw, out of the corner of his eye, the silhouette of a tall figure watching him from across the street, but when he looked directly, all he saw was the remains of a roof torn off by the wind, precariously propped against the wall of what seemed to be an abandoned warehouse. He shrugged and continued on his way.

At dusk, Andrei was walking along the promenade next to the city's seawall. Lost in thought, he observed the damage caused by the violent storm the previous night.

The noticeable stature of a man across the avenue had slightly caught his attention when he heard a loud crash just behind him. Someone had taken a hard fall off a bicycle right behind him.

The person who had fallen was a somewhat nervous-looking man, dressed in a raincoat with a hood and a face mask. Sunglasses completed the outfit, further concealing his face.

Andrei quickly turned around and, leaning slightly toward the fallen man, extended a hand to help him up. In doing so, the necklace with the statuette slipped out from under his clothes and hung on the iridescent cord, swaying in the air.

The stranger had a reaction that completely surprised Andrei. With a quick movement, the fallen man grabbed the statuette and, pulling hard, tore it from around Andrei's neck, causing it to fall onto the asphalt. The man clumsily tried to grab it but instead pushed it a few inches away.

Andrei reacted quickly and recovered the object.

—Hey, what's this? —Andrei almost shouted. —I try to help you, and you try to rob me?

—Listen to me, —the man gasped, his voice filled with concern. He seemed to have arrived in a hurry, either fleeing from something or trying to catch up to something. —There's no time to waste. You must give me that statuette.

An immense feeling of distrust overwhelmed Andrei in that moment. Could this mysterious man have been following him to rob him? That would explain why he was so heavily covered to hide his identity. But aside from apparently not carrying any weapons, there was something strange about him.

Something about the odd man felt familiar, perhaps his voice or his body's build. Andrei had a distinct feeling of déjà vu, as if he knew this person from somewhere or was reliving the same moment twice.

—Do I know you from somewhere? You sound familiar.

—There's no time for explanations. That object is dangerous, —the stranger warned, pointing at the necklace. —You must believe me. It will end your life. It will claim your mind and then your soul, Andrei.

—There's no time for explanations. That object is dangerous, —the stranger warned, pointing at the necklace. —You must believe me. It will end your life. It will claim your mind and then your soul, Andrei.

—How do you know my name? Have you been watching me? Of course, I won't give my necklace to you. I'd like to see what you plan to do about it.

Andrei clenched his fists, ready to defend himself if the man tried to take it by force. But the stranger's tone seemed more pleading than commanding, though it wasn't without a certain hint of menace.

—Please, Andrei. Don't make this more difficult than it already is. I don't want to hurt you, but I've hired two guys who will take the statuette from you by force.

—Then there's no doubt—you're a coward. Now that we're on a first-name basis, you know this item is valuable, and I'm sure you'll take it to sell it to some rich fool or...

—Believe me, Andrei. This isn't about money, —the stranger said as two men in black hoodies and sandals began approaching from a nearby street. They were also wearing face masks. Andrei noticed their presence and quickly tucked the necklace under his shirt while the stranger kept talking ominously.

—It's something bigger than us, —the stranger continued. —Something very dark that lies in the Atlantic and is connected to that statuette. Please, give it to me. It's for our own good.

A brief silence fell over the promenade next to the seawall. The only ones on the street were them and the two men in black, who were quickly closing in.

The sea crashing against the wall between the jagged rocks of the coast filled the air with tiny salty droplets. The streetlights had turned on automatically with the fading daylight, casting a cold white light on the pavement and the faces of the two men, who were now too close.

—Grab him! —the hooded man ordered his two henchmen.

Andrei took off running. He dashed across the avenue at full speed. He was no longer a young man, but his legs hadn't yet abandoned him.

He managed to put a decent distance between himself and the thugs, but the men in black hoodies were also tenacious, with the advantage of youth on their side.

The fugitive rounded the first corner, plunging into a bustling market. He bumped into several people, trying to weave through the crowd, but ended up accidentally knocking over several stalls of trinkets. He didn't stop running.

From time to time, he glanced back to see if his pursuers had lost sight of him, but the two thugs were still on his tail, their masked heads popping up over the horizon of people as they searched for him. With a sharp turn to avoid a very tall man standing in the middle of the street, Andrei finally made it out of the bazaar. He was startled to see that they were still chasing him.

Fortunately, Andrei spotted a row of taxis parked on the side of the street and threw himself, exhausted, into the nearest one.

—Where to, sir? —the taxi driver asked, looking at him through the fogged-up rearview mirror, not noticing the urgency with which Andrei had entered and locked the door.

—To the other side of the city, quickly!

The car started moving with an irritating calmness as Andrei frantically rolled up the window, watching through the rear windshield as his two pursuers ran toward the taxi. He couldn't contain a sigh of relief as the car pulled away, seeing the two thugs fade into the distance.

—Now I'm safe, —Andrei thought.

The street the taxi driver was driving on had the right of way at the next intersection, so he didn't slow down when he nearly hit a distracted pedestrian trying to cross first.

—Watch out, you idiot! —the driver yelled, honking the horn.

Andrei turned, curious to see who had risked their life in front of the vehicle.

His heart skipped a beat when he recognized, in the headlights, a man kneeling on the ground over a bicycle. He was wearing a hood and sunglasses. It was the leader of his pursuers. The kneeling man pounded the ground in frustration as his two henchmen joined him.

What interest did that mysterious man have in the statuette? Why was he chasing Andrei so relentlessly, even hiring two people to take the strange object from him? Andrei didn't know. He wasn't even sure if he wanted to find out. Was the man just a con artist or something more?

The taxi dropped him off at a café outside the city, near a gas station. Andrei took the opportunity to buy a pack of crackers and a jar of jam. His wife was traveling, and he didn't feel like cooking in his current anxious state.

A little later, Andrei arrived home. Although he was calmer, he cautiously looked around to make sure those men hadn't followed him. For a moment, he thought he saw the figure of a very tall man watching him from across the street, but after blinking and looking more closely, he convinced himself that no one was there.

"My anxious mind is playing tricks on me." He thought.

A few hours later, Andrei was feeling much more relaxed. After a long shower, he sat in the armchair in front of the TV.

He still had many questions in his head. The mysterious hooded man knew his name, so it was possible he knew where Andrei lived.

This thought threw him back into a state of anxiety. He grabbed the phone and called the police. An officer on the other end of the line listened to his story and informed him that two agents would be sent to his house to investigate the situation.

The officers arrived relatively quickly. After a brief interrogation, they left, promising to investigate his case. That gave Andrei some peace of mind, despite the fact that the two officers seemed a bit incompetent to him.

A phone call from his wife restored a bit of normalcy to the night. She informed him that she would be returning the next day, and Andrei was overjoyed at the news. They would be together again and go on vacation. He thought that would help him forget about his recent problems.

In a good mood, he decided to call his son, who was doing his military service in a distant province.

—Hey, Dad. What's up? What's going on? —came the young man's voice from the other end of the line.

—Hey, son. It's good to hear your voice, —Andrei sighed. —Things have been a bit tough with work lately, and it's been complicated trying to call you, but here I am, for whatever you need.

—Are you okay, dad? —his son interrupted, sounding worried. —You left me really concerned after what you told me when you called earlier. Is something wrong at home?

—What are you talking about? This is the first time I've called you today. Today and for the last three days. Who have you been talking to?

—What do you mean? You called me over an hour ago. I got really worried because it sounded like you were saying goodbye or something...

It's no wonder Andrei went to bed with his mind spinning. He barely slept, thinking that some deranged person was harassing him and his family.

With his wife in the capital, the bed and the room felt enormous and eerily empty. To make matters worse, a fierce storm broke out.

The next day, Andrei sat in his armchair to eat his toast with jam, happy about his wife's imminent return home. He turned on the TV with the remote and tuned in to a local news channel.

They were reporting on the damage caused by two consecutive nights of heavy storms along the coast. There was also news about the disappearance of a luxury yacht called *Odysseus* from the docks of Antilla, several dozen kilometers north of the provincial capital. The report stated that the yacht belonged to an important politician from the region and that the police were treating the case as a possible theft.

Uninterested in the news, Andrei took one of the toasts and spread jam on it, just as he had done thousands of times before. He wasn't even paying much attention to what he was doing. He bit into the slice as usual.

He instantly spat it out in disgust. The jam on the bread had an inexplicable, rancid fishy taste.

He checked the jar. According to the expiration date on the label, it was still good, so the jam should have been fine.

With some frustration, Andrei threw the jar of jam into the trash, thinking it must have been spoiled at the factory. He figured buying a bad jar of jam was just bad luck, a trick of fate.

Little did he know that what fate had in store for him was far worse and that in the coming days, he would be consumed by the desire to never have been born.

After a long week, Andrei was unrecognizable, both physically and mentally, as well as emotionally. In just seven days, he had been transformed into a shadow of the vibrant man he once was. It's astounding how a whole life can be destroyed and dragged to the brink of misery and madness in such a short time.

—What I'm going through is something I wouldn't wish on my worst enemy, doctor. I'm on the verge of ending my life.

Andrei was lying on the couch in the hospital's psychiatric consultation room, nervously fidgeting with a business card between his fingers. The doctor, a middle-aged man with a graying beard and round glasses, discreetly cleared his throat to get Andrei's attention. With a reproachful look, he pointed to a sign on the wall behind his desk that read, "SUICIDE IS NOT THE SOLUTION" in soothing blue letters, accompanied by a group of smiling young people.

—It was just an expression. But for the past week, I've been living in hell. I can't take it anymore, honestly.

—You can tell me everything. That's what I'm here for. To try to help you. Based on your symptoms, we can prescribe medication or even consider hospitalization if necessary.

—Honestly, being hospitalized wouldn't be such a bad idea. I have nothing left to lose.

—We'll see about that. Tell me about your current problems. What brought you here today?

—In the end, this, —Andrei said, showing the business card he had been playing with. —After all, it seems the old antique dealer knew far more than he let on. I went back to his shop several times during the week, but it was always closed.

—That's one of Mr. Sánchez's skills, —the doctor replied in a strange tone, —saying less than he knows. If he recommended you come, then your case must be quite serious. Can you give me some details about what you're experiencing?

—I keep having terrible hallucinations.

—What kind of hallucinations?

—I see, feel, hear, and dream terrible things. At first, it was small things. No matter how far I was from the coast, I smelled a strong scent of saltwater, and everything I ate tasted like rotten fish. Unpleasant things like that, but small details.

—Have you experienced any traumatic events recently?

—Yes, —Andrei's voice trembled. —Two, actually. My wife died in an accident while coming back from the capital. She was unrecognizable. I hadn't even finished mourning her when I got a call from the camp where my son was doing his military service. They told me he and two of his comrades had fallen into a pit. My son didn't survive the accident.

—It's likely that all of this triggered some kind of imbalance in your psyche, perhaps resulting in post-traumatic stress disorder. Do you know what I mean?

—Yes, I have an idea.

—Tell me more about your visions.

—As I was saying, at first, it was small, insignificant things. But then came the dreams... and the apparitions. Oh, my God, I see my wife and son, dead, everywhere. They appear to me both while I'm awake and when I'm asleep. In my dreams, the three of us are underwater. Each of us is holding an exact replica of this cursed statuette. They tell me I'll soon join 'Him,' that I'm one of His chosen ones.

Andrei stopped squeezing his hands and took a deep breath, but he couldn't calm himself.

—On several occasions, when I wake from those horrific nightmares, my bed is soaked in liquid. It's not sweat, nor is it urine, as you might think. It's seawater, and it's accompanied by bits of seaweed. You probably think I'm crazy. I'm not even sure of my own sanity anymore. I need help. I need to silence the voices. They whisper unimaginable things to me, and it makes my skin crawl.

—You said the object is a statuette? —the doctor asked.

—Yes, it's this. —Andrei pulled a small metal box from his shirt pocket and, with trembling hands, took out the mysterious object. —Look, I think I've thrown it away several times. But it always comes back. It always reappears somewhere in my house, as if it's alive. I've even started doubting whether I really tried to get rid of it, or if those were hallucinations too.

His futile attempt to calm his nerves faded, and Andrei began breathing heavily again.

—Soon after I found it, some men chased me to take it from me. At first, I thought they were petty thieves who somehow knew the object was valuable and wanted to steal it to sell. Now, I'm not so sure. I'm not even sure my senses can be trusted anymore.

The doctor's attentive gaze revealed a mix of fascination and unease. It was as if he were observing something extraordinary and wonderful, yet deeply terrifying and dark.

—Mr. Andrei, —the doctor spoke gravely, —you are perfectly healthy, but you've been cursed in a terrible way.

Andrei sat up on the couch, staring intently at the doctor.

—Look, I don't want to judge you, but I find it unorthodox that a person of science, with a supposed materialistic and pragmatic mind, would talk to me about curses. Seriously?

The doctor smiled enigmatically as he adjusted his glasses.

—Just confirm one detail for me, please, —the doctor said softly. —In your hallucinations, have you seen a man taller than normal, with completely black eyes?

—Yes, I've seen a very tall man, about three meters tall, staring at me with pitch-black eyes. I've also dreamed of a kind of giant worm or slug devouring people in a horrifying way. And the most shocking thing I've seen in my dreams is a... Wait, how do you know that?

Instead of answering, the doctor pulled a copper-colored fountain pen from his briefcase, adorned with strange symbols, and began scribbling something on his prescription pad. The object reminded Andrei of the antique dealer's magnifying glass.

—Mr. Andrei, we are at a crucial moment, —the doctor said, tearing off the paper and handing it to his patient. —Please, meet me this evening at this address. We have a unique opportunity on our hands, and it would be unwise to waste it.

Andrei took the prescription and looked at it on both sides. On one side was an elegant handwritten address in the city center. On the other, he recognized the same symbol he had seen on the antique dealer's suede gloves.

—Is this some kind of joke? —he nearly shouted in anger. —I came seeking medical help, and you give me some witchcraft... What kind of charlatan are you?

—Calm down, Mr. Andrei, —the doctor said firmly. —Have you noticed that since you entered this room, you haven't had any hallucinations? Am I right?

—Yes, now that you mention it...—Andrei calmed down and thought for a moment. —Here, I feel a peaceful atmosphere, doctor. I haven't felt this way in days.

Andrei smiled and almost cried from relief, though he didn't fully understand where it was coming from. It was as if the place itself exuded a protective sensation, guarding him against the forces that were slowly driving him insane.

—Even the irritating smell of saltwater is gone. Tell me, why do I feel so much better in here?

—Look at the anti-suicide poster. Do you see the emblem on the shirt of the boy in the center of the group? It's the same protective symbol I gave you. It's an ancient arcane symbol, older than humanity itself. It was created to ward off very dangerous entities that are beyond comprehension. That's why you're protected from harmful influences, at least to some extent... Please, don't get rid of it and meet me at the place and time indicated. As I said, we have a unique opportunity.

The doctor let Andrei sit in silence for a short while, giving him time to digest what he had just revealed. Then, the doctor politely dismissed him, signaling the end of the session and calling for the next patient.

After spending the rest of the morning and almost the entire afternoon sitting on a park bench, Andrei walked through the city streets. He was lethargic, lost in his own thoughts, walking like a zombie but with a fixed destination. He was heading to the address on the note given to him by the peculiar doctor.

Such was his state of distraction that more than one passerby approached to ask if he was feeling unwell. Curiously, for the first time in a week, he felt fine, free of hallucinations and terrifying, maddening sensations.

Finally, without even realizing how much time had passed during his sleepy walk, he arrived at the gates of the city library, the location marked on the small card. He reread the note, as he had completely forgotten the doctor's name. It only had the initials J.R. and the surname Hernán.

With this information, he inquired at the reception desk, where he was directed to wait in front of a magnificent oak door, intricately carved with low-relief arabesques. Andrei couldn't help but notice that the lines, seemingly running in random directions, subtly formed the same arcane symbol that was protecting him.

He sat on the wooden bench in front of the door and, for the first time since finding the cursed statuette, fell into a deep, nightmare-free sleep. He woke to the sound of footsteps echoing on the polished marble tiles.

—I'm glad you came, Mr. Andrei, —said the doctor as he quickly walked down the hallway.

This time, instead of his white coat, he wore black khaki pants and a gray wool sweater. He seemed genuinely happy and relieved to see Andrei.

—Come in, —he said as he opened the magnificent door. —We have a lot to discuss and very little time.

The walls of the office were completely lined with shelves filled with books. Some were modern bindings, while others looked ancient. The doctor sat behind an exquisite mahogany desk. With a courteous gesture, he motioned for Andrei to sit in one of the stately, leather-covered armchairs.

—Since time is of the essence, —Dr. Hernán began, —I'll be as brief and direct as possible. The object that has brought you so much misfortune is an Atlantean statuette. It was created in a very remote time, long before ancient Greece. It represents one of the aspects of Gloón, the God of Atlantis, also known as the Corrupter of Flesh. An entity worshipped thousands of years ago in the kingdom of Atlantis, back when it was still above water. Please, stop looking so skeptical.

—Atlantis? —Andrei said, both annoyed and surprised. —What makes you think my problems are related to an ancient legend?

—You're not entirely wrong. It could very well be a legend from ancient Greece. But in Plato's dialogues, *Timaeus* and *Critias,* he describes in detail the existence of a place called *A tlantis Nēsos,* or the Island of Atlas, as translated from ancient Greek.

The doctor pulled something from one of the desk drawers. He showed Andrei an ancient map.

—According to Platonic texts, it was an island in the middle of the ocean, which today bears its name. It had a military power that dominated the seas more than nine thousand years ago, long before Hellenistic civilization. The problem is, it's nearly impossible to determine if Plato's work was describing a fictional or real place, but recently it's been discovered that there was a massive island, almost a continent, in the middle of the Atlantic at a very remote time...

—What's your point? —Andrei interrupted. —I see you're very knowledgeable and probably some kind of sorcerer or something, but I don't see how this cursed statuette fits into all of this, or how I can get out of this hellish mess.

—Please, let me finish, —the doctor replied firmly. —In addition to being a psychiatrist, I also hold doctorates in History and Archaeology. For a long time, I was a professor at prominent universities in three different countries. My specialty is books on the occult and esotericism. Through them, believe it or not, I've been able to prove things that the average person's imagination couldn't conceive as real. All the information I have is crucial to your current situation. Tell me, do you only dream of your deceased wife and son, or do you see more than that?

Andrei calmed down a little and began to speak in a soft, monotonous cadence.

—I see a temple. A sanctuary submerged in the ocean, glowing with a sinister red light. Its structure and columns resemble ancient Greece, but I feel it's infinitely older. From inside, I hear a kind of call that pulses in my subconscious, even while I'm awake. Every day, I feel the urge to go to the sea, responding to that voice.

Andrei stopped speaking. His eyes seemed veiled by a blue mist, and his skin turned pale and clammy.

With a start, he returned to reality. He sensed a strange smell in the air, like ozone. The doctor, still seated behind the desk, was watching him with a very serious expression, his forehead beaded with sweat.

—Are you telling me the source of my madness is a temple at the bottom of the Atlantic?

—I prefer the term 'psychic contamination.' Gloón wasn't called the Corrupter of Flesh for nothing, —the doctor replied. —The temple you see is the prison where his physical body is confined. The statuettes are part of the mechanism to open the doors of that prison. The worm uses its mental influence to compel certain humans to find the keys and release it into this world.

—Look, this past week has been completely insane. I can't even tell what's real, a hallucination, or something entirely different anymore. And yet, what you're telling me doesn't make any sense. —Andrei crossed his arms, grumbling in his seat. —If what you're saying is true, and this Gloón...

—Gloón, —Dr. Hernán corrected as he went over to one of the bookshelves.

—Whatever, —Andrei continued. —If this Atlantean god has been imprisoned for nine thousand years, manipulating humans to release him, how come he hasn't found all the 'keys' and broken free by now?

—Very good point, Mr. Andrei, —Dr. Hernán said, still with his back turned as he handled something on the shelf. —I must tell you that, contrary to what is commonly believed, not all humans are the same. Some individuals possess characteristics, sensitivities, and abilities that set them apart from the rest of humanity and make them more susceptible to certain influences. I'm sorry to say that you have the attributes that have made you a target for Gloón.

Andrei huffed and shifted in his seat. Suddenly, the magnificent armchair didn't seem as comfortable.

—On the other hand, there have been people like me, since time immemorial, who have tried to keep the world safe from the clutches of these dark forces.

Hernán turned around and, to Andrei's astonishment, placed several small, finely carved pink crystal boxes on the desk. Inside, to Andrei's surprise, were exact replicas of the statuette on his necklace. He noticed that the same arcane protective symbol was engraved on the lid of each box.

The doctor returned to his seat behind the desk. He began pointing to the boxes, explaining the story behind each statuette's discovery.

—Five years ago, we found the *Laureth*, a wrecked fishing boat from North Carolina, 200 miles south of the Azores. It had been sunk for a short time. The reports said the crew had gone mad, and a mysterious explosion in the engine room sent the ship to the bottom. Inside, we found the figurine the crew had frantically mentioned in their final messages.

—This other one, —he lightly tapped the second box with his index finger, —was brought to me a few months ago by a desperate man. He told me about his visions, the sensations, the submerged temple he saw in his dreams. Not to mention the hideous worm that visited him in his nightmares. He lost his entire family and blamed all his misfortunes on the cursed image, which he brought to me. To this day, I regret not being able to save that man...

The doctor's index finger rested on the third box, which was empty.

—Some time ago, during one of my expeditions to the Dominican Republic, my team and I found a letter in a bottle on the north coast. It belonged to Karl H.G von Ehrenstein, captain of the U-29, a German submarine from World War I, which sank in 1917 under circumstances like the *Laureth*. None of its crew survived. They either drowned, died in mutinies, or went mad, including the captain. The trouble began after they torpedoed a British freighter, where they found one of the statuettes in the hands of a corpse floating among the wreckage.

Dr. Hernán paused thoughtfully.

—That letter was the clue to what could have been the discovery of the century, —he continued, —because the captain described in his letter the location of the sunken submarine. The coordinates, though imprecise, pointed to a submerged city which, according to the captain, was none other than Atlantis. If you don't believe me, I can show you the letter. I have it safely stored, but I doubt you understand German, let alone the captain's handwriting.

Andrei, confused, furrowed his brow and shook his head, lost in thought for a moment.

—And what happened next? Did you conduct an underwater exploration?

—It was the most exciting of my life. And also, the most disappointing, —Dr. Hernán replied, with a hint of nostalgic melancholy. —We moved heaven and earth to find the U-29 and Atlantis itself. My greatest ambition is—and remains—to seal Gloón in his prison at the bottom of the sea forever. He can only communicate with the outside world psychically, mainly contacting those who find these statuettes. He uses dreams and hallucinations to torment people until they lose everything, even their sanity, and are compelled to join him in his temple-prison.

The doctor took a few short steps around the office. His intense emotions were reflected in the tremor in his voice.

—In a certain forbidden book, —he continued, —locked away under seven keys at a university in the United States, there is a detailed description, among other greater horrors, of the characteristics of Gloón, the infamous being I'm telling you about. Had we found, during the exploration, the third figurine of Gloón, that monstrosity would now be cut off from the world forever.

Hernán stopped in front of the desk, gazing at the crystal boxes.

—I had given up on the mission until you appeared, —the doctor turned and stared directly at Andrei. —Give me the necklace, and you'll be free at last. The world will be safe from the danger of Gloón breaking free and exerting his malevolent influence over humanity, as he did in ancient times.

—How are you so sure there aren't more statuettes like these scattered across the ocean?

—According to the book I mentioned, there are only three. There's a lot of valuable, unknown information in apocryphal or heretical books.

—I see you're very familiar with this kind of thing, —Andrei said in a strange tone.

—Yes, I must confess, —the doctor replied after an uncomfortable silence. —So, what do you say?

The phone rang sharply, like a string of lightning bolts. Dr. Hernán answered the call and hung up after a brief, —Yes, I'm coming.

—I see you're hesitant. Will you hand over the object to seal Gloón? —the doctor said as he headed toward the door. —I'll leave you alone for a few moments. I hope that when I return, you've made a decision that will, of course, benefit us both.

Andrei stood up and began to pace around the office, trying to clear the whirlwind in his mind. A suspicion about Dr. Hernán started to form.

Andrei recalled the idea that the doctor could have been the hooded assailant from a week ago. But such a thing seemed impossible. Dr. Hernán's age, build, and physical condition were vastly different from that of the masked man. Moreover, the stranger had evoked a sense of déjà vu that the doctor did not.

Abandoning such suspicions, Andrei's eyes and attention eagerly settled on the title of a thick book with a colorful cardboard cover and pristine white pages, lying open on the desk. To his astonishment, he had seen it before, on the counter of the antique dealer's shop, the same day he found the statuette. When Andrei picked it up, he smelled the pleasant scent of a freshly printed book.

Andrei raised the new book to his eyes level.

"*Tachyonic Storms and Wormholes: Viable Methods for Time Travel?*" he read aloud from the title, stamped in large red letters on the cover. The title alone suggested that inside its pages were topics far too complex for an ordinary person like him.

The thought that he was caught in a whirlwind of immense forces, with him being nothing more than a puppet, struck him again with intensity. Pessimism enveloped him like a black cloud. He dropped the book onto the table. He heard the oak door open behind him.

—Excuse me, doctor, but even if I give you my statuette, I don't see how that will prevent Glo̒ón from sending his agents to retrieve it in the future. And after everything I've lost, I can't find a way to save myself either...

Hernán reentered the office and patted Andrei on the shoulder.

—That's why we need a good plan, —Dr. Hernán said.

—And the right tools, —echoed a voice with a strong Galician accent from the door, —and a brave man with the necessary attributes, willing to sacrifice everything to execute it.

Andrei turned, surprised.

The elderly antique dealer hobbled into the office and placed a metal briefcase on the desk. Using his black suede gloves, he opened the combination locks of the case. From inside, he pulled out a pink crystal box and a thick, old, unpleasant-looking tome. Its dark covers seemed to be made of leather, but Andrei had the uncomfortable feeling that the material had a more sinister origin.

—Although, to be completely honest, —Mr. Sánchez said with a note of sadness in his voice, —I fear that some sacrifices will be necessary, and salvation is never guaranteed...

He arrived at the lonely park, in the dead of night. He sat on the most distant and shadowy concrete bench. Still half-dazed from the effort, the heavy smell of ozone burned his nose.

He pulled down his hood and proceeded to remove his glasses and mask, revealing a face weathered by the coastal sun. A slight breeze ruffled his disheveled hair, like a nest of seagulls. He let himself fall onto the cold concrete bench, with his head down and a lost look in his eyes. Once there, he broke into silent sobs.

The only other people in the gloomy park were a teenager and her partner, walking a small dog on the grass. The stranger didn't care whether they noticed him or not. All he could think about was the family he would never see again.

The humid air seemed to encourage him to let it all out, crying like a newborn. He began with a sob. Then, unable to hold back the tears, he buried his face in his hands. The first drops of rain began to fall. The sky itself seemed to accompany him in his sorrow, shedding tears from the heights of the night clouds.

He lifted his head, noticing the increasing drizzle. He felt the raindrops soaking him from head to toe as he lowered his face again, but not before seeing the nearby streetlight flicker for a few seconds, taking on a strange greenish-blue hue. A heavy downpour was now falling on him. Yet, he didn't move from the cold bench.

He took a deep breath and prepared for the consequences of what he was about to do. He pulled two pieces of paper from the inner pocket of his raincoat. One of them was still smoking.

He held the sheets in his right hand. Within moments, the storm's rain soaked the pages, making the ink run and erasing the symbols drawn on them. A sudden gust of wind snatched the papers from his fingers, making them disappear into the night's darkness.

—Hey, buddy, do you need help? You're going to catch a cold out here.

The man on the bench didn't respond. He didn't even look up to acknowledge his concerned interlocutor. However, the person who initially seemed like a worried good Samaritan soon revealed their sinister identity.

The seated man was forced to raise his head again, puzzled by the sound of slow, sarcastic applause. With horror, he opened his tear-filled, rain-soaked eyes to see the eerie figure of his speaker standing before him.

It was the macabre giant that had appeared to him in his dreams. The ten-feet-tall titan clapped slowly and mockingly. He stood barefoot before the horrified eyes of the seated man. The latter was paralyzed by terror, unable to stop staring at the giant's face, which bore the same features as those abhorrent marble statuettes.

The giant, still clapping, began speaking again to the seated man, who could barely breathe from the unspeakable terror he felt toward the figure in front of him. That presence, which seemed to have escaped from the dream world, now stood before him, unbearably vivid.

—Bravo, Andrei. Bravo, —said the giant sarcastically, stopping his applause. —The old antique dealer and Dr. Hernán gave you the key to travel back in time. A tachyonic storm. Who would have thought that small, insignificant beings like you would someday be able to use such a power?

The giant shook his head with condescension.

—So, the big plan was to 'rob yourself' and take the last statuette," the creature continued. —You even hired some thugs to help you. Very clever. But I was watching you the whole time. There's no escape, Andrei. You belong to me.

The lights in the empty park flickered before going out, accompanied by an unnerving thunderclap. In the absolute darkness, the demonic figure that had come for Andrei continued speaking, standing in front of him.

—What was the goal? Did you hope to create some sort of parallel dimension where the current Andrei could be with his family, so your 'past self' wouldn't suffer the same fate? A timeline where your family is still alive, even if it meant breaking space and time?

The giant took a few steps and sat next to Andrei. He leaned forward, staring in the same direction as the terrified man. Then, still in his hunched position, the giant turned his head, his completely black eyes seeking the stupefied face of his victim.

—Cheap tricks like that don't work on me, Andrei. I can see the whirlwinds of time. Your fate has been set since the beginning of this universe. You will bring me the third statuette. You can't get rid of it or leave it behind.

Still talking, the giant stood up again, in the same spot where he had first appeared.

—You couldn't stop yourself. You failed to take the statuette. Your stupid plan failed, and soon the last thread of sanity you have will snap, and you'll become the tool of my will. You will retrieve the remaining keys, descend into the dark abysses to the doors of my temple, and you will set me free.

The giant's laughter mingled with the rumbling thunder.

—And you know what the best part is? —Gloón continued mockingly. —Your little time-travel stunt has provided me with two versions of you. So, when the "you" from the future frees me, I'll still have another version of you to make lose his family all over again.

—Why are you doing this to me? Why are you torturing me like this? —Andrei stammered, sobbing.

—Metal cannot be purified without fire. And fire hurts, Andrei, it hurts a lot. Don't you understand? It's all part of a process. You are special; that's why I've chosen you. You'll be part of the most glorious future.

The giant looked up and extended his arms under the pouring rain.

—My magnificent Atlantis will rise from the depths of the ocean, with a brilliance that will shock the entire world. So much knowledge, so many arcane secrets lost for millennia will resurface to lead humanity back to its peak of splendor, —the imposing figure began to levitate until it was floating two meters above the ground. —My chosen ones, purified by my hand, will stand at the right hand of my throne. The gods of Olympus will be nothing compared to what I will make of you, damn it! Rejoice, Andrei! Cry in pain now. Tomorrow, your tears will be of joy. Receive your future tears from the heavens themselves. Don't you feel their taste?

In the darkness that seemed to swallow the world since the lights went out, a lightning strike revealed an emptiness where the giant had been standing in front of Andrei. A grotesque laugh echoed from the shadows, making Andrei's heart lurch and the hair on his neck stand up.

He noticed, with unspeakable revulsion, that the rain falling on him was turning salty. He looked up at the clouds, hidden in the night's darkness, toward where the repulsive salty deluge was coming from. And there, under the electric light of a lightning bolt, he saw the blasphemous image of two enormous, abominable eyes in the stormy sky. That disgusting rain wasn't water; it was the tears of those monstrous entities, high in the void.

Gloón's macabre laughter faded with Andrei's screams of terror.

He found himself curled up on the ground. Some park-goers had approached out of curiosity and concern. They even seemed to feel some pity for Andrei, perhaps thinking he was a poor, mentally ill man who had escaped someone's care.

Was it real, or part of a horrible hallucination? Was it a dream or a nightmare? It was becoming increasingly difficult for him to distinguish what was real and what wasn't.

No. He was awake, unfortunately, because, despite having his eyes wide open and being surrounded by real people, he continued to hear the voices of his deceased family. His wife and son whispered in his ear that they were with the Lord of Atlantis and that soon his soul and body would be with them too.

—Sir, do you need help? —asked a girl with golden eyes, who didn't seem at all affected by the torrential rain. But Andrei trembled, covering his ears, lying on the ground in a fetal position.

—Shut up! Stop tormenting me, please! Stop talking to me! You can't be here anymore! —Andrei screamed, pressing his hands to his ears. The tormented man wasn't speaking to the kind people around him, offering their help. Even though he could see them, they were strangers to him.

His desperate pleas were directed at the voices that he wasn't supposed to hear because the people speaking with him were dead. And that hurt him deeply.

Andrei stood up, like a comatose patient rising from their bed after an eternity in a stupor. His physical appearance and psyche were far removed from the Andrei of not long ago.

Once on his feet, he staggered forward a few steps. The small group around him stepped aside, fearful that Andrei might be a dangerous madman. A little later, he wandered the dark city streets like a zombie, shouting aloud at the voices multiplying in his mind, terrifying every passerby he encountered.

With his hands over his ears, pulling at his hair and stumbling, he managed to reach a public phone. He felt that the end of his life was near. His conscience demanded one last act, more for comfort than salvation, like a final wish granted to a death row inmate.

He needed to hear that voice, if only one more time. The real one, coming from outside, not from within his mind. The one he knew better than any other, the one that had always made him so happy, but now, he only heard it in the whirlwind his consciousness had become.

—Is that you, dad? —he finally heard it again. The voice of the little person he had held in his arms at birth.

—My son! You don't know how happy I am to hear your voice again, —he said, struggling to control the tears running down his face.

—Yes, me too. Is there something important you want to tell me?

—I just wanted to know if you were okay. It's been so long since we talked because it's been hard to get in touch with you.

—Yes, that's true. I'm doing well here. You know, it has its tough and strict side, but you get used to it. How's Mom?... Hey, are you crying?

—Hmm?... Yes, son. I'm crying with happiness. Your mother is in the capital, but she's okay for now. Listen. Whatever happens from now on, I want you to know that I love you very much, and I'm sorry I wasn't there for you when you needed me most. Someday, we'll be together again, the three of us. Who knows, maybe in a better future or...

—Dad, you're scaring me. Why are you saying these things? Is everything okay at home?

—What? Yes... of course. Why wouldn't we be okay, son? It's just that I've been a bit sentimental lately. Old people's stuff. Don't forget, every day that goes by, your mother and I are eagerly waiting for your return. Stay away from high places... or deep ones. Be careful when you're in the mountains.

—Now, seriously, you're worrying me. There's something you're hiding, and you're not telling me. What are you talking about? What is all this about?

—I love you, my son. Always remember that...

A thunderclap rumbled through the air with a booming roar. The lightning struck very close, causing the streetlights to flicker and the phone call to cut off permanently. Andrei, filled with anger and sorrow, began shouting and pounding the phone and the graffiti-covered walls of the booth, cursing Gloón and the voices, which he now heard more strongly than ever before.

Sitting on the ground in front of the phone booth, Andrei cried uncontrollably as passersby looked at him with disgust. It was starting to rain again. Andrei kept hitting his head and screaming, cursing the voices that wouldn't stop tormenting him over and over again.

Until he heard a voice that didn't come from within him, nor from the shocked pedestrians on the sidewalk, nor from those taking shelter at the bus stop. It emerged like a faint echo from the depths of his shattered mind. He perfectly recognized that malevolent, eternally mocking voice that, with a loud.

—Silence! —quieted all the other whispering specters, as if it had authority over them.

—Come on, it's time to recover the rest of the keys," the familiar voice of the giant echoed in his subconscious. —Let's go to Dr. Hernán's office. Thanks to my previous 'messenger,' I know he's hiding the statuettes there. That damned bookworm and his old friend, that meddling Iberian antique dealer, have already interfered too much in matters greater than themselves. The first thing I'll do when I'm free is pay them a pleasant visit...

—I won't let you...

—I'm tired of your heroic side! —the giant roared. —I belong to a race of gods. When we arrived here, your species hadn't even emerged yet. We have so much power that your tiny human brains mistake us for deities. It's time to show you a glimpse of that power.

Andrei felt as if lightning struck the top of his skull. An intense electric current coursed through every nerve, causing all the muscles in his body to spasm. The man stood up and began walking with long strides. He no longer controlled his physical body.

When Andrei regained consciousness, he was standing in front of the oak door to Dr. Hernán's office. In the dim light, he could make out the glowing lines that formed the protective symbol on the wood. This time, he didn't feel the usual sense of peace and security, but discomfort and even pain. The control that Gloón exerted over his body was too great. The arcane symbol repelled the impure creature he was becoming.

—Let's see what a predestined body is capable of when touched by the grace of a god, —Gloón's voice resonated in his mind.

With a violent kick, Andrei ripped the door from its sturdy frame and hurled it across the room until it crashed into the desk with a deafening sound. Both objects were completely destroyed in a chaos of splinters, metal, and papers.

Walking stiffly, the puppet of flesh advanced toward the shelf from which Dr. Hernán had taken the small pink crystal boxes. With a swipe, he knocked the books off the shelf, revealing a safe embedded in the wall. The protective symbol glowed on the steel door.

The fingers of the man controlled by the Lord of Atlantis sank into the metal as if it were wet cardboard. With a fierce tug, the door was ripped off, and the contents of the safe were exposed. Andrei crushed the crystal boxes as if cracking almonds. He pocketed the two statuettes in his raincoat and left the room quickly.

Andrei's next moment of consciousness came as he was untying the ropes of a luxury yacht. He barely managed to read the letters on the hull of the boat: *Odysseus*. *Antilla Port* emerged from the depths of his memory but was quickly lost again in a maelstrom of chaos and darkness.

—Come on, I want you to savor this moment with all your senses, —Gloón said.

The smell of saltwater flooded Andrei's nose. This time, it wasn't a hallucination. His eyes took in the infinite horizon of the deep ocean and the ashen sky.

—Gloón, I swear you will pay dearly for everything you've taken from me...

—Why do you cling to such a mediocre life, in such an inferior form, when you are on the brink of apotheosis? With me, you will cease to be a mere mortal. Together, we will lead your species out of ignorance and usher in a new era of greatness under the regal reign of my will.

—What greatness could you possibly offer, you worm...?

The figure of the giant manifested, floating in the air before Andrei.

—To be honest, —Gloón said mercilessly, —all the fun of torturing you for a week would have vanished if I had just said the simple phrase, "COME TO ME".

With those words, something like a switch seemed to activate within Andrei's subconscious. What remained of his being and personality was plunged into the abyss of nothingness.

All emotion vanished from the man's face, replaced by a cold, expressionless mask. His eyes became two glassy, dark blue bubbles where his pupils should have been. His skin took on a bluish-green hue, covered in a sticky, sickly mucus. The body, which had still maintained some athletic form despite the past week's torment, twisted into obscene and repugnant curves.

The Corrupter of Flesh rejoiced in his work. He could have done it earlier, but Gloón was perverse and took sadistic pleasure in watching his psychological tortures slowly break humans. Soon, this entire world would be his to enjoy at will.

—Now, let yourself be embraced by the cold arms of the ocean. Come to the Temple of Wisdom in the city of beautiful plazas. Bring the keys, for what is now inert, and dark will soon be filled with strength and light.

At the snap of the giant's fingers, what had once been Andrei jumped overboard and sank into the deep, dark waters.

The creature swam for hours, immune to the cold and crushing pressure, until it finally reached the submerged city.

Guided by the call of the Lord of Atlantis, it arrived at the Temple-Prison and floated before the massive circular door. Three empty niches awaited the placement of their respective keys.

The transformed being took the first statuette from the pocket of its raincoat and, with repulsive, undulating movements, placed it in the receptacle pointing westward. The marble glowed with a sickly greenish light, and a mechanism activated in the circular door, causing a large ring to rotate, pulsing with strange and ancient symbols.

The creature swam to the eastern niche and placed the second key in it, which lit up with the same repugnant green color. Another ring, studded with symbols, began to spin on the door.

Inside the Temple, Gloón vibrated with a joy he hadn't felt in millennia. He was particularly happy because the human's time-traveling antics would allow him to torture Andrei again in even more creative ways. Plus, he now had two bodies of predestined humans at his disposal. If he had accomplished so much with just one and while imprisoned, he trembled with anticipation at what he could achieve in freedom, and with two of them. Only the placement of the third key remained.

Fighting against the water current generated by the fast-moving mechanism, what had once been Andrei swam to the niche at the top of the door. He reached for the last key at his neck. When the slimy, mucus-covered skin touched the statuette, it lit up with an intense white light. The creature's dead eyes gleamed clearly in the abyssal darkness.

—Gloón, Lord of Atlantis, Corrupter of Flesh, you, despicable worm! —the voice resonated in the mind of the imprisoned god. —Underestimating humans will be your downfall.

It was Andrei's voice.

—With the wisdom accumulated over generations, Dr. Hernán and the antique dealer Sánchez crafted a ritual to alter the characteristics of the statuette. They modified the complex spell of the key so that instead of opening this door, it reinforces the seal, preventing your vile influence from seeping out of your prison.

—Impossible! How...?

—My journey to the past was to make the switch. That whole chase scene was just to deceive you. I had already swapped the statuette for a harmless replica during my 'fall.'

While you were watching the Andrei of the past, I, shielded by a reinforced version of the arcane protection symbol, applied the modified spell to the statuette. Accept your defeat, Gloón!

Andrei brought the white key closer to the receptacle.

—Wait! —Gloón cried out in desperation. He sensed that the humans' plan had a flaw, but the gravity of the situation prevented him from seeing it clearly. He had to buy time. —If you seal me now, the bond I have with you will be severed, and you will lose the benefits of my blessing. Your body will be destroyed by the cold and pressure of the ocean. You won't survive to see your wife and son again.

Andrei hesitated, holding the key just centimeters from the niche.

—Gloón, you killed my wife and son and tortured me with hallucinations of their mutilated bodies for a week. That suffering tempered me like fire tempers steel. That's why I was able to endure the impossible agony of the tachyonic storm. I may die here, but the Andrei of the past will be free from your cursed influence. Some sacrifices are necessary to ensure the future.

—That's it! —the Lord of Atlantis screamed, finally realizing the flaw he had been seeking. —The key from the future...!

But Andrei, with a swift movement, inserted the modified statuette into the receptacle. The central circle of the door began to spin in the opposite direction of the others, and its symbols glowed with white light. Slowly, the mechanism reversed its rotation, and all the symbols shone white. The door flashed brightly and then became still and dark.

"Now, Corrupter of Flesh, you are isolated from the outside world, imprisoned in your Temple of Wisdom. You will be the laughingstock and disgrace of your kind!" Andrei thought just before the cold and pressure of the Abyss overtook him.

"We're back with breaking news. In the early hours of this morning, local authorities were called to the city library following a report of a break-in. Late last night, the night guard noticed the intruder as they were fleeing the scene and immediately reported the case to the police."

"There was a forced removal of two archaeological marble figurines from a safe belonging to Dr. J.R. Hernán, along with significant damage to historical documents dating back to World War I. So far, the well-known doctor has not provided any further relevant details regarding the missing items."

"Meanwhile, Senator Paulo R. Santeiesteban's recreational yacht was also stolen from the docks at Antilla Port during the early morning hours. Eyewitnesses claim the boat, famous for its speed, headed east. The whereabouts of the *Odysseus*, the name given to the politician's vessel, remain unknown. There are concerns the yacht may have sunk due to the bad weather."

"And speaking of bad weather, two consecutive nights of strong storms have left..."

Andrei pressed the on/off button on the TV remote. It was too early for bad news. He'd already had enough the day before when some thugs had tried to mug him in the street to steal the curious statuette, he had found that morning. To make matters worse, his son had received a strange phone call during the night. Luckily, his wife was returning today from the capital.

He answered the phone while preparing some toast with jam.

—Yes? Who's speaking? Oh, Mr. Sánchez, the antique dealer... Oh, great, you found information about the statuette I showed you. What? Do one of your clients is interested in buying it? And he's willing to pay a good sum for it? Very well. I'll stop by your shop later, after I take a walk on the beach. You never know what the tide might bring after a storm. See you later.

Andrei hung up the phone and took a bite of his toast with jam. It was delicious.

The elderly antique dealer hung up the phone.

—It seems that our friend from the future was successful in his mission, —commented Dr. Hernán as he tapped on the lid of a small pink crystal box resting on the counter.

—Let's hope so, —the old man replied as he put on his black suede gloves with the strange silver symbol on the back.

The antique dealer hobbled to the back of the shop and returned with a heavy metallic suitcase. He placed the object on the counter and began turning the dials on the locks.

—If our friend in the present agrees to sell us his piece, it could be quite useful for throwing off any potential interested parties. The material to make replicas is almost impossible to find, —said the doctor, handing the small crystal box to the antique dealer. —Not that I'm complaining, but what a "gift" our friend from the future has left us.

The locks on the suitcase snapped open.

The old man took the box and held it up to the light. Inside was a marble figurine with a cord.

—Sometimes we find things, and sometimes things find us, —said the antique dealer with his thick Galician accent, placing the box in the metal suitcase. —At this point, dear doctor, you should know that in this line of work, salvation is never guaranteed, —he added, closing the suitcase with a click.

THE BLACK BONES GARDEN

At the edge of the city, exactly at its center,
lies the vast garden of the black bones,
the only place, hidden in the dreamlike Carcosa,
where the yellowed skies allow to see the Universe.

It is there, under a hundred moons and a thousand dying stars,
when three times shines Algol over the ashen place,
that the Yellow King sings his ephemeral eternal lullaby,
he picks the finest fruits, and in the wind releases seeds.

With a sorrowful step, the alchemist wandered through the labyrinthine paths of the Garden of Black Bones. His emaciated body was wrapped in tattered rags, worn out by the rigors of a thousand journeys. His feet, tired and wounded from traversing immeasurable distances and countless dimensions and planes of existence, dragged along the paths paved with fine gray gravel, leaving no trace on the strange material.

Someone with a slightly weaker will, with knowledge a bit less solid, would have broken long ago. However, the motivation of this man had the burning intensity of a star and the unyielding rigidity of an obsession. He would not stop until he achieved his goal.

The cadaverous figure stopped and moved his head. An eventual witness might have thought that the decrepit man was observing the bewildering black mounds scattered randomly throughout the place.

Those things were worthy of attention.

The cadaverous figure stopped and moved his head. An eventual witness might have thought that the decrepit man was observing the bewildering black mounds scattered randomly throughout the place.

Organized in an impossible balance and of varying heights, they were composed of elements resembling bones, but with a preternaturally polished texture and an abyssally black color. Within each of the bones, strange and variable-colored points of light floated lazily.

A good part of the piles was undoubtedly of human bones; the rest were, without a doubt, of alien origin. However, all the sets had one characteristic in common: all the skulls had the same perplexing format, with a smooth plate and no facial holes, and three openings on the top of the skull.

Nevertheless, the alchemist was not looking at those alienating objects. His eyes were closed. He was listening.

In the air of the garden floated a hypnotic, soft, and disturbing sound, like the death song of a blue whale making the moon's regolith vibrate. It was a lullaby that, at the same time, contained no words and was intelligible in all the languages of the universe. It was the song of the Lord of Carcosa.

Guided by the sound, the alchemist corrected his path.

After what seemed like an infinite march, the twisted paths led the wanderer to the central esplanade where, surrounded by countless piles of bones, stood the Yellow King. Wrapped in his golden cloak, the monarch looked at the sky with his head and face covered by the hood of his robe. His radiance tinged the nearby dark bones with a yellowish hue.

He sang his alienating lullaby.

—Hastur! —croaked the alchemist, and his voice echoed in the place like shards of obsidian falling from a cliff. —I have followed the deceptive trails, found the forbidden tomes, and deciphered the arcane contents to find your city.

I have traversed the maddening paths of Carcosa to find your garden. I have twisted the flows of Time to arrive at the right moment. I have traversed, distorted, and manipulated Creation itself to find you here and now.

—Do you know, little mortal, —the words of the Yellow King formed in the mind of the Alchemist, shaking every fiber of him, —why I keep the sky of this place clear and unobstructed? —the imposing figure kept his gaze on the heights, where the stars shone coldly. —It is to know when the time of harvest arrives. —He pointed with an uncomfortably long index finger to a point in the universe. —The shine of Algol always tells me when the fruits are ready to be picked.

The golden monarch slowly lowered his hand and turned toward the newcomer. His presence was terrifying, capable of disintegrating the consciousness of the weakest or least prepared. His chest, where the cloak did not cover, was a chaos of strips or perhaps bandages that beat at a strange and unnatural rhythm. Between the hood and the mask, where the face should have been, opened an abyss of darkness. His voice, soft and alienating, resonated again inside the man's skull.

—Show me your seed, the one that guided your steps here, and tell me what you desire, little mortal. Forbidden and profound knowledge? Pleasures beyond understanding? I see in your eyes that material wealth has ceased to interest you long ago, so tell me, what does your heart yearn for?

—What does my heart yearn for? —the man bent down, looking at the ground, putting his hands inside his rags. —My only desire...—the alchemist abruptly raised his head and stared at his interlocutor. His eyes gleamed with fury, —is revenge.

Silence floated over the eerie garden.

—She was joyful, —growled the alchemist, —intelligent and beautiful, until she found your cursed "seed." At that moment, her mind was poisoned with the nefarious yellow sign. In no time, the desire to reach this cursed city consumed every one of her thoughts, and nothing else mattered to her. She sacrificed everything to find her way here.

The man's teeth ground with rage. What shone on his face might have been bitter tears.

—My first sin was not trying to stop her. After losing her, I searched for her tirelessly. I followed her trail to the decaying halls of Carcosa, but when I found her, she was nothing but a shadow of what she had been. At that moment, I swore that the one responsible for this misery would pay dearly for the pain he had caused.

The gaunt figure stood tall.

—With blind fervor, I began seeking the means to carry out my revenge. I pursued the hidden knowledge in forbidden texts, infiltrated libraries that were more like fortresses to take notes directly from the cursed pages of the Necronomicon, got lost in the burning sands of Arabia to read the moldy papyri hidden in the basements of the Nameless City, and breathed radioactive dust while consulting the forgotten records in the endless towers of Korad's Dead City. I gathered knowledge that few can boast of possessing, and yet I found nothing capable of harming a being like you in the slightest.

The man was foaming with rage as he spoke.

—Until my journey caught the attention of someone I least expected. One night, at the foot of the mighty Kadath, while washing the blood from my hands in a small iridescent stream after a disastrous raid to obtain a grimoire in the Dreamlands, I was granted an audience with Nyarlathotep himself, and from the mouth of the Crawling Chaos came the instructions on how to make you pay for what you took from me.

The alchemist pulled from his garments a mask of impossible colors and a long black dagger. Symbols of destruction and ruin that glowed intensely ran along the curved blade of the weapon.

Slowly, the man covered his face with the mask and shouted.

—It was hard to obtain the materials and even harder to enter the deep workshops of R'Lyeh to forge these objects, but there is no cost, no matter how high, that I am not willing to pay to punish you for what you took from me.

—Ah, little mortal, —softly said the Yellow King, —everyone who finds their way to Carcosa does it driven by the intense desire for knowledge. I do not force anyone to come, much less to stay. If your beloved decided to join my flock, it was of her own will...

—Silence! —the alchemist roared, pointing the sharp dagger at the golden monarch. —To forge this blade, I used your cursed seed and the same material from which the flutes that keep the Lord of All Things asleep are made. The destruction and ruin spell embedded in its edge was taught to me by Nyarlathotep himself. With it, I will silence you until the end of this Creation. Your time has come, Hastur!

—And what makes you think, little mortal, —the Lord of Carcosa purred, —that you are capable of such a feat?

Like a golden lightning bolt, the tall figure of the Yellow King traversed the distance between him and the alchemist. His implacable arm pierced the man's chest until his long-fingered hand projected out from the back of the gaunt figure.

Then the primordial being felt something he had not experienced in eons. Surprise.

The form that was beginning to disintegrate in front of him was not made of mortal flesh but of smoke and fine dust. He tried to withdraw his arm, but a strange and firm force prevented him.

A bony arm appeared from his back and stabbed the long black dagger into Hastur's chest. With a swift step, the alchemist stood before the Yellow King and pushed the weapon in up to the hilt, cutting the strange straps that flailed desperately in the air. The man growled through gritted teeth as he twisted the blade within the wound.

—Return to the depths of Azathoth's dream, from where you should never have emerged.

In the paroxysm of his triumph, the alchemist felt the Yellow King cover his face and head with an enormous and implacable hand, and with a single fluid movement, enveloped his entire body in the golden mantle.

—Teaching mortals how to create material shadow illusions. Ha, ha, that trickster Nyarlathotep is getting more mischievous every day...—were the last words the man heard in the soft voice of the Yellow King as he felt his entire being consumed by a golden flame of cosmic intensity.

With ultimate horror, the alchemist perceived how the mask that covered his face vaporized the flesh beneath it until it reached the bones of his skull, which were already being deformed and remolded, while his most precious memories and emotions were sucked out by an overwhelming force, ripped from him forever.

He tried to scream, but he no longer had a mouth.

—Ah, —Hastur finally exclaimed, opening his right hand and observing the three small tear-shaped stones in it, —the best fruits always produce the best seeds, —he blew his breath over the objects, and the yellow sign glowed within each one. —Now, it's just a matter of planting them and waiting for the next harvest...

With his left hand, he pulled the dagger from his chest and made three parallel slashes in the night air. The cuts opened wounds in the very fabric of reality, through which different lights and scents seeped. With care and delicacy, the Yellow King placed an object in each of the slits, then closed them with a gentle swipe of his long index finger.

Once the sowing was complete, he threw the dagger high into the air, where it disintegrated into tiny pieces of gray gravel that fell gently, merging with the pavement of the garden's paths.

The Lord of Carcosa began to walk, dragging his long yellow mantle. He still sang his disconcerting lullaby.

At the site of the confrontation, there remained a new pile of black bones, with a preternaturally smooth surface.

It was impossible to determine whether the shimmering points dancing within those remains were reflections of the stars in the eternal sky or the last embers, remnants of the flame that had burned in the soul of that being, driving him to follow the forbidden paths that led to his doom.

Now it no longer mattered; the garden had gained another pile of black bones, and the next harvest had been planted.

The Yellow King continued his march through the labyrinthic paths of Carcosa.

GLOSSARY

Areíto: Sacred ceremonies of the Taíno indigenous people. The ceremony consisted of songs and dances accompanied by the sound of indigenous instruments.

Aroma: Also known as ***marabú*** (*Dichrostachys cinerea*), it is a species of thorny shrub native from Africa, Southeast Asia, and Australia. It is an invasive species on the island of Cuba, where, having no natural enemies and being difficult to eradicate, it has spread over large areas, invading farmland and pastures. Land overtaken by this plant, as well as the tangled mess formed by these shrubs, are called *aromales* or *marabuzales*.

Batey: Name given to the villages of the native Indians of the Caribbean islands. Typically, it consisted of a single row of structures around a circular plaza. Nowadays, the term *batey* is used to refer to small towns around sugar mills.

Behíque: Among the Taíno Indians, a priest and healer. Shaman.

Bohío: hut, made of wood and branches, reeds or straw.

Cacimba: In Cuba, this term refers to natural cavities in limestone rocks caused by erosion. They can become quite deep and accumulate water at the bottom. They are also known as sinkhole.

Caguairán: A tree of the *hymenaea* family, also known as *quiebrahacha*, characterized by its very hard wood.

Caney: A circular hut made from palm leaves or straw.

Catey: A small parrot.

Cazabe: Pie or bread made in various parts of America with cassava roots.

Conuco: A plot of land that the Taíno Indians dedicated to farming.

Criollo: A person born in the territories of the Spanish colonies in the Americas. They could be the child of Spaniards or people of African descent and were not necessarily mixed race. The term is used to indicate that the person was born in the Americas, meaning they did not immigrate to the continent. It is not used as a derogatory term; on the contrary, in many Spanish-speaking territories, it is a source of pride.

Guayabera: A men's shirt decorated with two vertical bands of small pleats or embroidery; with two pockets on the upper part and two more on the lower part. It can have short or long sleeves. In Cuba, it is the national men's attire and can replace a suit in formal ceremonies.

Jutía: A rodent mammal of the *Capromyidae* family, common in the Caribbean. Depending on the species, it can be similar in size to a rat or a rabbit.

Mayohuacán: A wooden slit drum played by the Taíno indigenous people. The instrument was played during sacred ceremonies, most notably the *areíto*.

Majá: (*Chilabothrus angulifer*) A non-venomous constrictor snake endemic to Cuba and some other

Caribbean islands. It typically grows up to four meters in length and 25 cm in diameter in the middle of its body. In Cuba, the word *majá* is generally used to refer to any large snake.

Mogote: A prominent, isolated hill. The term is often used to describe such geographic features in the Caribbean, in islands like the Dominican Republic, Cuba, and Puerto Rico. These are limestone hills that usually appear in regions with tropical or subtropical rainfall.

Pitirre: (*Tyrannus cubensis*) giant kingbird, species of songbird. It is currently endemic to Cuba and is threatened with extinction.

Romerillo: (*Bidens alba*) A very common herbaceous plant in Cuba. The flowers have a ring of white petals around a yellow center. It is considered a medicinal plant.

Taíno: Pre-Columbian indigenous peoples native to the Caribbean.

Villas: As part of the colonization of the island of Cuba, the Spanish founded permanent settlements called *villas*. Among the first seven were the *Villa de San Cristóbal de La Habana* (now Havana) and the *Villa de la Santísima Trinidad* (now Trinidad).

This book is part of the *Silex Draconis* project, which is dedicated to the production and promotion of Fantasy, Science Fiction and Horror/Terror material. Here you will find fun stories that transport the reader to worlds far from everyday routine.

You can follow us on our social networks:

Silex Draconis

www.facebook.com/profile.php?id=100092486635754&mibextid=ZbWKwL

@silexdraconis

www.instagram.com/silexdraconis

@SilexDraconis

www.youtube.com/@SilexDraconis

www.ingramcontent.com/pod-product-compliance
Lightning Source LLC
LaVergne TN
LVHW010552160826
845677LV00013B/3096
* 9 7 8 6 5 0 1 1 8 3 4 9 7 *